center ice

A CORRIGAN FALLS RAIDERS NOVEL

Cate Cameron

Entangled Publishing, LLC
2614 South Timberline Road
Suite 109
Fort Collins, CO 80525
Visit our website at www.entangledpublishing.com.

Crush is an imprint of Entangled Publishing, LLC.

Edited by Alycia Tornetta
Cover design by Jessica Cantor
Cover art by iStock/Massonstock

Manufactured in the United States of America

First Edition May 2015

Chapter One

– KAREN –

The squirrel attacked on the sixth day. Five days of peaceful, almost solitary running, and then…carnage.

Well, that might be a little strong. But those little guys have *sharp* claws, and I was wearing shorts. Also, I had no idea what to do. I'd been running along just fine, concentrating on my breathing as I started up the steep hill, and then there was a blur of movement, a painful scratching on my leg, and I looked down to see a pair of beady little rodent eyes staring right back at me from halfway up my thigh.

I may have made a noise, maybe something like a panicked giraffe. And then I possibly did a strange little dance, trying to stomp hard enough to shake the squirrel loose. The movement just made him hang on even tighter, digging his claws farther into my exposed skin. "Get off," I yelled at him. "I'm not a tree!"

"Stand still." The voice was confident and male, and my inner feminist wanted to stomp a little harder just to show that I wasn't taking his orders. But standing still kind of made sense, so I froze, then peeked back over my shoulder. I recognized the guy, of course. He'd been the only other person I'd ever seen in the park this early in the morning, circling around the same route I used. About my age and a pretty good runner. Very fit. I tried not to notice how he was even *better* looking up close and hoped that in addition to being gorgeous he was also good with rodents.

"He just jumped on me, for no reason," I said. I guess I didn't want this guy to think I'd been provoking the squirrels? "Don't hurt him," I added. I was remembering some of the teenage boys I knew, assholes who'd probably take an incident like this as an excuse to prove their manhood with violence and gore.

The guy ignored me. He scooped a stick up from the side of the path, about three feet long and almost as thick as my wrist.

"No, don't hit him!" I wondered if I'd be able to outrun the guy with a squirrel firmly attached to my thigh.

He continued to ignore me. He came in close and brought the stick right up to the squirrel, like athletes do when they're lining up for a hard swing. But instead of pulling the stick back, he edged it down a little, slow and steady. "She's not a tree," the guy said, and there was maybe the hint of a laugh in his voice, as if he knew he was echoing my ridiculous words. "Come on, little guy. Back to the forest." The stick kept moving, and the squirrel put one forefoot on it and then the other. He was still staring at me, and I started to wonder whether he was trying to communicate.

My babies are trapped! I need your help! Or maybe something less immediate: *developers want to destroy my habitat; you must STOP them.* But probably he was just a crazy little rodent. When the stick got as far as his hind legs, there was a moment when it really seemed like he might be about to make a leap farther up, fighting his way onto my shorts—spandex, thankfully, so I didn't have to worry about him burrowing beneath the fabric—but instead he flicked his tail, spun around, and leaped off me. He scrambled up the nearest trunk and started this weird chirping, staring down at us in outrage.

"He's cussing you out," the guy said.

"Not me! He *liked* me. He's swearing at you."

"Yeah, probably," the guy admitted. He sounded like he was used to people swearing at him, which made no damned sense, because he was gorgeous and a hero. He crouched down and looked at my thigh. "No blood, but you've got some scratches. Looks like they're swelling up a bit. Are you allergic?"

"To squirrels?" I squinted at him to see if he was serious. "How would I know that? I mean, I've never had a reaction to squirrel scratches in the *past*, but…"

"Guess you're about to find out." He straightened up. His shoulders were really wide, and I wondered if I'd underestimated his age. His face seemed young, but most guys my age were still pretty skinny. He wasn't fat, for sure, but there was more muscle on him than I was used to seeing. And possibly I'd picked the wrong time to notice that, because he was looking at me as if he thought maybe I was going into shock or something. "You okay?"

"Yes," I said automatically. I took a careful step forward

along the path. "Doesn't hurt."

"You should rinse it off." He frowned. "Maybe. I mean, I'm not a doctor. I have no idea what you should do. But if you want to rinse it off, I can take you to the creek."

"There's a creek?" Five days in this park with no squirrel attacks *and* no knowledge of a creek. Apparently day six was all about exposure to new things.

"Yeah. There's a path to it just up here."

"I don't want to interrupt your run…"

"I can walk you back to the fountain, if you'd rather."

I hate myself at times like these. It's not weak to take a little help, and it doesn't mean I'm pathetic and needy if I let someone do something for me. But sometimes it's like I'm psychologically unable to accept assistance. "No, I'm fine. I'll go rinse it off in the fountain, but I don't need help." At least I was self-aware enough to realize how stupid that comment was. "I mean, I appreciate your help. Before, with the stick… that was excellent. And I'm really glad you didn't hurt him. But I'm okay now."

His stare was almost as intense as the squirrel's, but with him I got the feeling he was trying to receive information, not send it. "Okay," he finally said.

He watched me as I started walking, and I gave him a little wave and said, "Thanks again," then turned resolutely and started jogging. The scratches didn't hurt, but they *were* pretty itchy. I wondered how many people were walking around this world with an undiscovered allergy to squirrel scratches. I kept jogging until I was sure I was out of the guy's sight, and then I slowed to a walk.

Attacked by a squirrel.

It was like picking a scab, and I knew I shouldn't do it,

but I let myself imagine how I'd tell the story to my mom. She'd already have heard about the cute boy, of course, and she'd probably have been bugging me to talk to him. "You're so shy, Karenina," she'd have said. For the record, my name is Karen, *not* Karenina, and my mom was the one who named me, so you'd think she of all people would have respected her own choice, but apparently not. Mom had been a dancer, and I was named after a famous Canadian ballerina, which was fine, but apparently my mother had realized too late that the ballerina was elegant and graceful *despite* her name, not because of it. But Mom had never seen me as anything but beautiful, and she'd apparently decided to give me a more glamorous nickname to match. "Talk to him, Karenina. What's the worst that could happen?"

That's what she would have already been saying, and then when I told her about the squirrel, she'd have laughed and been excited, and scolded me a little for turning down the help. "If a handsome gentleman offers you assistance, why not take it?"

Once, in real life, I'd responded to a similar statement by pointing out what had happened to *her* when she'd let herself be taken in by a handsome gentleman, when she was only a couple years older than I was then. She'd frowned, then leaned forward and kissed my temple, hard. "I got *you*," she'd said fiercely. "I have no regrets."

By the time I got to the fountain, I was crying, thinking of the conversation I'd never get to have. I splashed some water on my face, first, and tried to get myself under control. Then I hoisted my leg up and rinsed off the scratches. They were nasty-looking, bright pink ridges with a thin white line down the middle of them. I poked at them because it felt better to have pain on the *outside* of my body, then splashed some more water on my face and headed out of the park. I was tempted to run again and wear off more of my negative energy, but I thought I'd better go find an antihistamine in case this squirrel allergy turned into a real problem.

When I got back to the house, Will was awake and in the kitchen. "Do you want breakfast?" he asked. He was eating a bowl of cold cereal, which I could easily find for myself, so it was sort of a weird question. I wondered what he'd have said if I'd asked for bacon and eggs or waffles or something. But he was my father, at least in an accidental-sperm-donor sense, and I guess he was trying to take care of me.

"I'll have something later. Do you have Benadryl?"

"Allergies?" He sounded concerned, but I had no patience for that bullshit.

"Nothing serious. I always get them this time of year. Not that you'd know about that." I smiled sweetly and shifted around a little so he wouldn't be able to see the lines on my leg. "So, is there Benadryl somewhere, or should I add that to Natalie's list?" Natalie was Will's wife, mother of his *other* children, and it seemed to work best if we kept communication with each other in written form.

"I'll check the master bathroom," Will said, setting his bowl down on the counter. "The kids don't have allergies, so it wouldn't be in theirs."

"Of course no allergies," I agreed. That would be a flaw, and imperfections were not allowed in this household. I was tempted to find a way to expose them to angry squirrels just to test the theory, but it seemed like a pretty complicated plan would be required.

I followed Will out to the bottom of the staircase and

waited for him there. I'd never been upstairs in this house. I mean, I'd only lived there for about a week, so it wasn't a huge deal. My bedroom and a small bathroom were in the basement, food and the doors to outside were on the main floor...that was all I needed. And absolutely all I wanted. These people were strangers, and there was no need for me to see their bedrooms. Not unless I was putting squirrels between their sheets.

Will came back downstairs with empty hands. "I couldn't find anything," he said. "Is it bad? Do you want me to drive you to the drug store?"

I shook my head. "No, I'm fine," I said pathetically. I actually was; washing the scratches in the fountain had been a really good idea, because they were way less puffy and itchy than they had been.

"I'm sure Natalie can pick something up for you later today, if you just tell her what you need."

Another sad nod. "Okay." I turned and took a few steps toward the basement stairs, but I stopped when he said my name.

"*Are* you okay?" he asked, moving closer. "I don't just mean the allergies. Overall, I mean. Natalie and I were thinking that you might want to talk to somebody." He must have seen the expression on my face, because he stopped walking. "I mean, we're both here for you, of course. But if you wanted to see somebody else...a professional...we could set that up for you. If you wanted."

"Because of what? Because I'm some sort of deviant or something?" I couldn't believe these people. "Seriously? Why don't *you* all go to 'a professional'? You could talk about your compulsive need for perfection. Or what it's like to have a kid you never bothered to meet suddenly show up on your doorstep."

"Maybe I should." It was seven o'clock in the morning, but he already looked tired. "I could go with you, if you wanted. Maybe Natalie, too, or even the kids. We're in a strange situation here, Karen, and there's nothing wrong with getting some help with it."

And there it was again. Getting help. But if I hadn't taken it from the hot runner, I was *not* going to take it from some dried up old therapist. "If you guys need help, go for it. But I'm fine." I whirled and stomped down the stairs to the basement, keeping my head carefully turned so he couldn't see my face. Realizing that a messed-up situation was messed up did *not* mean that there was something wrong with me. The rest of them could cruise around with smiles painted on their faces if they wanted to, but I wasn't going to lie that way. My mother was dead, I was living in small-town hell with a father I'd never even met until the day before the funeral, and his whole family hated me. A therapist wasn't going to help with any of that. *Nothing* was going to help with any of that.

I pulled my phone out and punched the familiar codes in, then held it to my ear. The voice was familiar, light and easy. "Hi, Karenina. I'm going to be a bit late tonight. If you go to bed before I get home, sleep tight! I'll see you in the morning."

A simple message. My mother's last words to me. And they'd been a lie. Not deliberately, of course, but she hadn't seen me in the morning. She'd never seen me again.

My phone asked me if I wanted to delete or save, and I hit save, then replayed the message. I tried to pretend it was real. I closed my eyes, lay back in the bed, and imagined I was back at home, in our funky little apartment in the city. I was sleepy, so I'd go to bed early, and when I woke up the next morning, I'd see my mom.

I played the message again, and again.

And then I opened my eyes. My imagination couldn't change reality. I couldn't go to the past. I was stuck in the present. And I wasn't sure how the hell I was going to get through the future.

Chapter Two

- *TYLER* -

"Move it, MacDonald! You need to be faster than that!"

I forced my legs to keep moving, driving forward over the smooth white ice. I was keeping up with my line mates, but the coach was right; I needed to be faster.

I put on enough speed to finish the drill a few strides ahead of the rest of my line and then I bent over, my stick braced on my knees as I gasped for breath. I didn't look up when I felt a body run into the boards beside me, and I knew it was Winslow as soon as I heard his ragged breathing.

"Out of the way," Coach bellowed at us, and we managed to push ourselves off to the side of the rink just as five other heavily padded players charged past the goal line and slammed their gloved fists down on the ice. I straightened up and forced myself to watch number 52, the center, racing back to the other end of the ice. I'd need a stopwatch to be sure, but I didn't think he was quite as fast as I was. He might end up being my replacement, but hopefully he wasn't going to push me out of my spot quite yet.

"He's not a playmaker," Winslow said from beside me. He knew me well enough to know who I'd been watching. "He doesn't have your instincts."

That would be really comforting, if it were true. Speed and strength could be developed, and Christiansen, the rookie center, was almost two years younger than I was; if he was nearly as fast and strong as me *now*, he'd almost certainly be faster and stronger by the time he was my age. But an instinct for the game was something that players either had or didn't; it could be developed, maybe, but not created. But I wasn't sure Winslow was right about Christiansen's instincts. "Let's get him drunk tonight, and see how fast he is when he's skating with a hangover."

Winslow grinned at me. He was my best friend, and he knew that I wasn't quite *that* much of an asshole. "You'll be fine, Mac," he said and glided a few feet away.

I'd be fine. Yeah, if I could just do as I was told, turn myself into a hockey machine, focus on the game, not let myself get distracted by that girl in the park, the way her hair moved as she ran, the way she'd been a bit of a smart ass about the allergies thing, the way—

Then the coaches were yelling again, and we got back to work. I didn't have time to think about anything but drills and skills for the next couple hours, and that was fine by me. It was weird to be feeling like I was over-the hill when I wasn't even eighteen yet, but if I started thinking about all the young guys coming up behind me, it tended to freak me out.

I was showered and just pulling my clothes on after practice when Coach Nichols waved me into his office. I followed reluctantly; there was no way of avoiding the conversation, but that didn't mean I was looking forward to it.

I was the fourth person in a room that had originally been a storage closet, and there were only three chairs: one behind the coach's desk, and two on my side, where my father and my agent sat impatiently. They'd been in the stands for the practice and had obviously been comparing notes.

My agent, Brett Gaviston, didn't waste time on formalities. "I need to see more out of you, Tyler. If I'm going to get you where you want to be, I need you to put at least a little effort in. I can't just carry you to the NHL."

I wanted to point out that *I'd* been the one sprinting around the ice for the last two and a half hours while he sat in the stands and let himself be courted by the dads of other players, but I kept my mouth shut. I'd long ago learned that there was no point.

"You need to be *dominant*," my father said. "Even in practice. You should have been carrying that team around on your back. This is the Ontario Hockey League, Tyler. It's the biggest supplier of NHL talent in the world! Every kid in that locker room wants to get to the show, and every kid out there is working for it. Are you?" He gave me a disgusted glare. "This ain't the bush leagues, son."

The bush leagues were the only place he'd ever played himself, but somehow he was an expert on all things hockey. But, again, there was no point in me opening my mouth.

"You need to understand that I put my reputation on the line with every player I represent," Mr. Gaviston said. "If I recommend you to a team, if I *sell* you to a team and you go down there and you're lazy and uncommitted to the game, *I* look bad. I don't want to look bad, Tyler."

"You were supposed to be keeping in shape over the summer." My dad squinted at me as if trying to see the muscle definition beneath my clothes. "That was the deal when I let you stay down here. You did the clinics, so that was something, but what were you doing the rest of the time? If you'd been at home, you know you'd have been working your ass off. *Travis* was working his ass off, and he's only thirteen. I expect you to be a leader, to blaze a trail for him, not stink up the family name with your *total* lack of hustle!"

"I wasn't concerned with Tyler's performance," Coach Nichols said quietly. The other two glared at him impatiently, like he didn't know what he was talking about, but neither one of them had the balls to contradict him openly. He was one of the most respected coaches in the league, a thirty-year veteran who consistently produced winning teams and high draft picks. My dad and agent cut on him behind his back, but they didn't say much to his face. Coach shrugged nonchalantly. "He's doing extra dryland training on his own, on top of the regular team workouts. He's come out well on all our pre-season testing: cardio, strength, even flexibility. Practice is practice, and I saw a good effort today; when the games come, Tyler will be ready."

It caught me by surprise, I guess, because I suddenly had a weird tightness in my throat. The coach knew I was working; he knew I was doing the best I could. It was a great feeling, but one that was almost completely destroyed when my dad turned his frown on me. "You should stop doing the extra training," he said, as if it was the most obvious thing in the world. "Work harder when you're with the team, when people can actually *see* you. Just because there's no scouts in the stands right now doesn't mean that they aren't going to hear about what's going on. And we need them to hear good things."

"They'll hear good things from *me*," Coach said firmly, and that shut my dad up because a coach's recommendation was incredibly valuable. "Tyler's training program is team-approved, and I don't want changes made to it without running it by our staff." He stood up, and even in that tiny, dingy office, his authority was clear. He might have been wearing a ratty pair of training pants and a ten-year-old team jacket, but he made Mr. Gaviston in his fancy suit look like a little kid playing dress-up. "Thanks for your time, gentlemen. Tyler, you'll make sure the rookies understand that watching game film is *not* optional, right?" There might have been a twinkle in his eye when he added, "And have a good run tomorrow."

The rookies were mostly gone by the time I made it back to the dressing room, but I wasn't too worried about it. Toby Cooper, the alternate captain who shared the leadership duties with me, had already made it crystal clear that they'd damn well better do everything the coaches said if they wanted to have a prayer of sticking around, and I'd backed him up. We were still pre-season and hadn't made the final cuts yet, so the rookies were being really well-behaved. I might have to sit on a few of them later in the year, but for now, they were good. I was pretty sure the coach had made the comment just as a way to remind my dad and Mr. Gaviston that I *was* a team leader, whether they thought so or not.

"You want to do something?" Winslow had stuck around and waited for me, but I could tell he knew the answer to his question before I said it.

"Nah. I'm just gonna…" I waved my hand vaguely toward the doors of the arena. Winslow knew what I meant. We'd never had a long conversation about it, but he knew how much meetings with my dad always bugged me. I needed some time to decompress afterward.

"I think we're playing Xbox at Sully's, if you want to come by later." Tim Sullivan was over eighteen and was allowed to have an apartment instead of billeting with a local family, so we mostly hung out there. My billet family, the Cavalis, were nice enough, but there wasn't a lot of privacy. Not that we needed privacy to play Xbox, but doing *anything* at the Cavali house was sometimes a bit like being an animal on display at a zoo.

"Thanks. I'll call if I run out of things to do."

"And we should go out tonight, right? Not too many curfew-free nights left, man, and so many lovely ladies looking for a little attention." He grinned. "I know, you've always managed to fit them into your schedule even during the season, but it's a lot more convenient when you don't have to worry about getting into your own bed by ten o'clock, right?"

And that was another thing I didn't really feel like dealing with. "I'll call you, okay?"

Winslow let me go, and I headed out to the parking lot, the heat of the day hitting me like a body check after the cool of the rink. I saw my dad waving at me from the front of the arena, but I kept my head turned away. I didn't need a second dose, not right then.

My pickup was big and old and ugly, and it burned both gas and oil like it was trying to heat the world all by itself, but it was mine. I shut the door behind me and laid my head back against the seat for a second. I would have liked to have stayed like that for a while longer, but I could imagine my dad's progress across the sun-baked parking lot, and I peeled out through the back exit before he could get too close. I'd turned off the ringer on my cell phone so I was free, at least for a while. Now, if I just had something to *do* with that freedom.

Chapter Three

I took my time getting showered and dressed, hiding in the security of my little basement home. Eventually I heard sounds of activity from upstairs. Will had probably left for work, but the rest of the family had hauled their lazy asses out of bed and were starting their day of leisure and perfection. I'd missed my chance to have breakfast without company, and since eating with them pretty much turned my stomach, I decided to wait a while. There was a full-sized fridge behind the bar in the basement rec room, and I wondered about stocking it with some milk and fruit so I could have meals on my own. The closer I could get to self-contained living, the better, as far as I was concerned, and I was sure the others would share my sentiments.

But it might not *look* right, and that would slow them down. They could justify me having a bedroom in the basement: it had been their spare bedroom for years, there was lots of natural light, and it didn't make sense to move any of the kids out of *their* bedrooms just to move me in. Minimal disruption, that was the goal. Keep everything normal, just the way it always has been. Let's all just try to ignore the fact that there's a *whole new person* suddenly living in the house.

"Karen?" I heard Natalie say from the top of the stairs. She seemed to be following the same rules I was about not trespassing on the other's floor. I appreciated her reticence, but still decided to ignore her and hope she'd go away.

No such luck. Her voice was a little closer when she said, "Karen!" and I poked my head out the door of my bedroom. She was standing halfway down the staircase, leaning over to be able to see me.

"Hi."

"Morning!" Her face was as cheerful and dishonest as her voice. "We're making waffles. Want to come up and have some?"

"Oh, no thanks. I already ate."

Natalie's face tightened a little. "Will said you hadn't." Not quite calling me a liar but pretty damn close.

"Huh," I responded. It's amazing how often refusing to communicate will actually work and get people to leave you alone.

But not in this case. "Why don't you come up and have some waffles?"

"I'm actually just on my way out. My allergies are acting up, and I was going to walk down to the drug store and get something for them."

She took another step down the stairs, looking concerned. That was a bit of a backfire; I'd been looking for guilty retreat, not guilty advancement. "Do you need me to drive you? The drug store's downtown."

"I was going to go to the one on the hill," I clarified.

She gave me a weird look. "That's even farther. That's clear across town."

Which was pretty much the point. "'Across town' doesn't mean too much in a place this size. I'm used to walking places, in the city. I'm not a fan of this rural car culture you guys have going on. You shouldn't have to drive everywhere."

She looked like she was about to argue, but then the forced smile was back. "A crusade. Okay. Enjoy your walk. But it's already getting hot out there, so if you get tired, give me a call and I'll come pick you up."

She turned around and headed back up to her wonderful children, who had probably dutifully prepared the waffles by now. I could imagine them, all wearing matching aprons, their blond hair carefully combed and tied back, mixing their wholesome ingredients with whisks instead of a mixer. The batter would be from scratch, of course, with a little family secret (nutmeg!) mixed in. The twins, Matt and Miranda, were almost eighteen, so they'd be in charge of the stove. Little Sara was only fourteen, so she shouldn't touch something so *dangerous*. She'd be washing fruit, and maybe cutting it up, but only with a table knife in order to protect her precious fingers. Crushed food was fine, if the alternative was even the *chance* of harm to dear, sweet Sara. They'd all smile and agree with that sentiment, and Matt would probably ruffle Sara's hair, or tweak her ponytail or something. Then he'd carefully wash his hands again before touching any food. Not because there was even a chance of dear Sara's hair being dirty, but just because that was the proper way to do things.

I'd rather get heatstroke.

Which I almost did. Before I left the city, my best friend Lindsey's mom kept going on about how nice it would be for me to be out in the country for the summer, away from the awful heat. I think it was literally the only bright side she could see to anything that was happening to me, and she was trying to be positive, so she said it *a lot*. And I think possibly she was high, because the heat today was as bad as anything I'd ever felt in the city. My short sundress that had seemed so light and airy when I put it on was hanging wetly off my body, and my feet were sore and swollen inside my sport sandals. Not a drop of a breeze, either. I had to walk across a bridge, and I looked down at the river beneath, all sludgy and green at the end of a long, dry summer, and I was seriously tempted to jump in. I'd end up looking like the creature from the black lagoon, but at least I'd be cool.

But going home like that, bringing my algae-covered self to the house of perfection? No. That would not be appreciated. So I kept walking, dodging into any patches of shade I could find, and finally made it to the air-conditioned sterility of the drug store. There was only one mall in town, and it was dark and full of stores for old people. All the new development was up here on the hill, big box stores separated from each other by endless parking lots, the asphalt softened in the heat. I tried not to think of all the funky boutiques mom and I had shopped at in Toronto. Maintaining my personal style was going to be a bit challenging out in the sticks.

I picked out some allergy pills just so I could say I'd bought them, browsed listlessly through the aisles while my sweaty skin chilled, and then headed for the cash register. There was a cluster of girls in front of me, probably about my age, deep in conversation.

"I can't even imagine," a tall brunette said. "It must be *so* awkward."

"And Miranda said she's a total bitch, too." The shorter brunette seemed absolutely thrilled with this news. I was getting a weird feeling in my stomach. How many Mirandas could there be in a town this size?

"She's just going to live with them forever?" A cute little blonde asked. "Aren't there, like, boarding schools or something?"

"Mr. Beacon's trying to be a good guy," the tall brunette said with a careless flip of her hair. "You know how he is."

"Yeah," the blonde said. There was something in her voice that made her seem not quite so cute anymore. "The whole *town* knows how he is. My mom said he's probably got a couple *other* extra kids scattered around. She says if he doesn't, it's a testament to the powers of birth control."

The cashier smiled as she handed over their change, and the girls headed out the door, tossing their hair and laughing happily. I stared after them for a little too long, I guess, because the cashier sounded kind of snotty when she said, "I can help you now."

I shoved the box of pills toward her and burrowed through my backpack to find my wallet. I could feel the tears coming, but I blinked hard and looked up at the ceiling and bit the inside of my cheek, and I made it out of the store without embarrassing myself. And then once I was outside, I started walking fast, and the moisture on my face might have been tears or it might just have been sweat. If I had to choose between being pathetic or gross, I'd take gross.

By the time I was across the wide parking lot and onto

the sidewalk, I'd managed to change some of my mortification into anger. I was angry at the girls in the drugstore, at Miranda for talking about me behind my back, at my so-called
father for…for *everything*. What's so hard about keeping it
in your pants? Natalie might not be my favorite person, but
she was pretty and took care of herself, and clearly loved
her husband and family. What kind of a guy can't be satisfied
with that? Is it just some pathetic male ego thing that makes
them sleep around? Was Will like some of the sleazy guys
I'd avoided at my old school, keeping an actual score of the
number of people they had sex with? It was disgusting, and
I wanted to stay as far away from it as possible.

So there I was, in the heat, sweat-crying, angry at Will
and all the pathetic men like him. I was charging down the
street, covering some ground, but I really wasn't sure where
I was going. That was probably a metaphor for something, I
figured, but it didn't seem like anything that applied to my
current situation. The part about not knowing where I was
going certainly fit, but I couldn't find a way to pretend that I
was covering any ground. In the metaphorical world, I was
bogged down in a swamp even murkier than the river I'd
crossed earlier.

Or possibly I was being a bit melodramatic. Why the
hell should I care what a bunch of shallow strangers thought
about me? I sure shouldn't care what they thought about my
so-called *father*. Maybe he was as much of a slut as they said
he was, but that wasn't my problem. It wasn't like I'd ever
thought he was a good guy. I kept walking fast, but I was
pretty sure I wasn't crying anymore.

It took me a while longer to realize that I'd been walking in the wrong direction, heading away from the house

instead of back toward it. But I didn't want to be the idiot who stopped short on the sidewalk, whirled around, and then started walking the opposite way, so I kept going. I was hoping I might find a store or something that I could pretend I'd been heading to all along, but I was on the outskirts of town by now and all I saw was an auto parts distributor and some place that seemed to center around farm machinery. But I kept walking until the sidewalk ended.

I was trying to decide whether to keep going or cross the street and go back along the other side when a navy pickup swerved to a stop in front of me. I had about a second of being scared, and then a familiar face appeared. He'd pulled himself out of the driver's side window and must have been sitting on the door as he looked at me over the roof of the cab.

"Hey," he said. "You running away from another squirrel?"

I desperately wished I wasn't bathed in sweat and dust from the road, but I did my best. "I'm not sure… It might have been the same one."

"You want me to drive you somewhere? You know, for safety."

"I'm not sure that getting into a truck driven by a strange male qualifies as 'safe,' technically."

"I'm not really all that strange." His smile was slow and unbelievably sexy. I wondered just how much I smelled; I was sure my feet were toxic, but if I kept my shoes on, how bad would the rest of me be? "Where you headed, exactly?" He looked at the road in front of us. "There's just farms out there… You going to one of them?"

Well, that was awkward. "No. I was just walking. I got a bit lost, I guess. I'm new to town."

He nodded as if this all made perfect sense to him. "I

don't have A/C, but it's not bad with the windows down." He treated me to another grin as he added, "Come on, little girl; I'll give you some candy."

I knew it was stupid, but I just didn't care. I was hot and tired, and following the rules had gotten me stuck in this ridiculous excuse of a life, so maybe it was time to break a few and see what happened. "Yeah, okay," I said. I strode over to his passenger door, and by the time I got there he'd slid back into the cab and leaned over to push the door open. It was a strangely gentlemanly gesture, and I felt even worse about my totally disheveled state. "I may smell," I admitted as I climbed in.

"Good thing the windows are open, then." He raised his eyebrows at me. "So, where to?"

"I honestly don't care," I said. "I'm just killing time."

He nodded thoughtfully. "I've got the afternoon off. You want to go swimming?"

"*Yes*." It was simple and honest. "Yes, I really do."

"All right, then." He carefully pulled out into traffic, then said, "Buckle up. I'm a terrible driver."

It caught me by surprise, and I laughed. "I've never heard someone admit that before."

"No point in denying it," he said cheerfully. "I'm a damn menace." Then he glanced over at me and shifted around so he could extend his right hand. "Tyler MacDonald, squirrel tamer and chauffeur from Hell."

I wiped my palm as subtly as I could on the skirt of my dress, then shook his hand. "Karen Webber. Damsel in distress, apparently." And for the first time in quite a while, I meant it when I smiled at him and said, "It's nice to meet you."

Chapter Four

- TYLER -

I had no idea what I was doing. I mean, okay, she was cute and female, so I was probably doing *that*, just like I always did. But it felt different this time. More innocent.

I'd only ever seen Karen wearing workout clothes and covered in sweat. Not that I had anything against hot, athletic girls wearing spandex, and I guess she was pretty sweaty this time, too, but the dress was a nice change. Made me think about running my hands up her legs, of course, but I managed to put that out of my mind, at least temporarily. She'd thrown me off, talking about how she might smell, and just being normal and friendly instead of what I was used to from girls. She was different, and I liked it.

But I guess I should have been paying a bit more attention to her instead of to myself, because when I turned off the highway onto the rough dirt road, she asked, "Where are we going?" and her voice was tense.

I had no idea what the problem was. "To the lake? To go swimming?" I tried to sound neutral, not like I thought she was crazy.

"We're swimming in a lake?"

"Is that all right?" She stared at me like I was an alien, and it made me nervous. So I started babbling. "You know the Dead Sea Scrolls? We learned about them in ancient history class. But I missed the first class, and the teacher kept mentioning them afterwards, and I thought he was saying the dead sea-squirrels." And that was probably enough of that weirdness. "I was just thinking, you know—there won't be any lake-squirrels to worry about. They died back in ancient times."

"We should stop talking about squirrels." She had a nice smile, especially when she was trying to hide it.

"Sorry, yeah, I guess it's a traumatic memory for you. You're right, it's best to forget."

I pulled the truck over at the same spot I always did, a little grassy clearing with trees on all sides. I had no idea who owned the property, but whoever it was didn't seem to mind the occasional swimmer. I turned off the engine and said, "Just over the hill." She didn't look totally convinced, but she climbed out of the truck anyway. She was really careful to lock her door, even though both of our windows were still wide open. Strange girl.

And maybe she was thinking that I was a little strange, too, because she was watching me as if she thought I might pounce. I had no idea what her problem was, now. "I don't have towels, or anything," I said, sounding defensive even to myself. "Sorry."

"That's okay," she said. She still sounded a bit weird, but she followed me when I led the way along the sandy path up to the top of the hill. From there, we could see the lake, and she seemed to relax a little. Maybe she'd been back on that took-a-ride-from-a-homicidal-maniac thing and was relieved that I hadn't lied about the lake, at least. "It's so deserted," she said, sounding surprised.

"Yeah. On the weekends, there might be a couple more people, but it's never all that busy here. People want to be at the public beaches, with snack bars and bathrooms and crowds." She still didn't look too convinced. "Shit, is that where you thought we were going? Somewhere busier?" I should have known. I liked coming here, but most people, and definitely most girls I knew, wanted to go somewhere more public, somewhere to see and be seen.

"I didn't really have any idea," she said, and she sounded like she meant it. She started down the hill toward the lake. "But this is perfect. It's beautiful."

"Yeah. I like it here. I'm not a huge fan of crowds." Which was true, but was way more than I should be saying to some girl I barely knew. I was supposed to be confident and popular and outgoing, not a crowd-phobic recluse. But she didn't seem too put off by my admission, and we scuffed along through the sand until we hit the band of smooth rocks down by the shore. "There's a shallow part over there," I gestured, "with warmer water. It's pretty cold out deeper."

We wobbled over the beach rocks and made our way to the little cove. I realized that I'd never brought a girl here before, and I was glad that she was wearing practical shoes; heels on these rocks would have been brutal.

I kicked my flip-flops off and pulled my shirt over my

head, dropping it down to the rocks, and only then noticed that Karen was standing totally still, staring out at the lake. Once again, I had no idea what she was up to.

"I'm going to rinse out my dress," she blurted out. "I'll swim in it, I mean. Because it's sweaty and gross." She looked a bit desperate. "It's repulsive."

I honestly hadn't given a lot of thought to what she'd wear in the water, but apparently she had. "Okay," I said carefully. I dropped my wallet and keys on top of my shirt and figured it was time to get the conversation back onto more solid ground. So I said, "Don't let me lose those. It'd be a long walk back to town." Then I started toward the water, walking carefully but easily on the shifting stones, and hoped she'd just follow after me without more weirdness.

But apparently I was being too optimistic. When I was about thigh-deep, before I made the final, critical commitment to the cool water, I turned around and saw her still standing on the shore. "You okay?"

"Yeah." She shrugged her backpack off onto the ground. "Just building up my nerve. You know, for the cold."

"It's not that bad," I said, and I waved my fingers through the water in what I hoped was an encouraging way. I wanted to swim, not drive this strange girl back into town. "On a day like this, it's perfect."

She seemed to believe me because she started toward the water. I turned back around and looked at the horizon, but I could hear her wading toward me. She was slow at first but sped up as she went, and when she was just about level with me she flopped forward, no grace or style whatsoever, just falling into the lake with a splash. Then she headed confidently out into the lake, her arms cutting smoothly through the water, and I was following before I'd even thought about it.

I had almost caught up when she suddenly dove deep. I could see her through the clear water, skimming along the bottom like a mermaid, and I don't think I would have been totally shocked if she'd stayed down there forever, maybe turning around to wave good-bye before disappearing into the cool depths.

But she eventually came back up, and I guess I startled her by how close I was. I grinned. "When you were being weird on shore, I was worried that maybe you didn't know how to swim. But I guess you do."

She didn't say anything, just took a deep breath and then ducked back under the water. She swam right underneath me, and I was tempted to dive down to join her. I wanted to touch her skin and see if it had been cooled by the water or if it was still warm. But mostly I wanted to talk to her more, figure out who she was and what was going on with her. So I followed along on the surface, and she eventually came back up and stared at me.

I had no idea what we were doing, but I was ready to experiment a little. I started off toward the middle of the lake; we were in Lake Huron, the opposite shore far beyond the horizon, so it wasn't like I thought I was actually going to get there, but it felt good to have a goal. And Karen followed right alongside me.

I finally stopped, and she started treading water beside me, giving me a look as if she wanted me to explain the game I was playing. Of course, I had no idea, so I shrugged. "No-body here. Just us." I should have had a better explanation, something that would tell her what a rare treat that was for me.

She obviously wasn't quite understanding. "Okay, if you're going to drown me and bury my body in the trees, you should just get it over with. You know?"

I had no idea what to say. "If you think there's a chance of that, why the hell did you follow me out here?"

"I didn't think there was. But then you said we were alone, and it just... I don't know." She ducked back under the water, but I understood what she was doing, now, finding a little solitude down there until she was ready to deal with me again.

Or, I guess, until she ran out of oxygen.

When she finally bobbed back to the surface I said, "Karen, I promise not to drown you."

She was ready for that, and added, "Or kill me at all. Or rape, or torture, or—"

"No crimes," I said quickly. "No assaults. No unwanted physical contact of any sort. I promise."

She squinted at me. "Of course, that's exactly what a torturing-rapist-murderer would say, isn't it? I mean, with a list of sins like that, I don't think you'd have to worry about a little lying."

"Those aren't the sins on my list," I said. And I didn't want to get into all that, so I waved my arm toward the shore, defaulting back to my tour guide persona. "Down that way is the public beach. Sand right to the water, and all the conveniences. And there's a kids' sports camp over that way. That's where I worked this summer, off and on. Beyond that is mostly trees. A few cottages, a few small beaches like the one we're at, but otherwise, just forest."

She was obviously bowled over by the sudden tidal wave

of information, but she found her balance and said, "That's nice. In Toronto we have Lake Ontario, but it's not like this. Almost all developed, along the shore."

"That's where you're from? Toronto?" I'd known she was from somewhere different, but not *that* different. "Damn. How'd you get stuck up here?"

She ducked back under the water again. I got the message, and when she surfaced I didn't press her for an answer to my question. But I couldn't think of what else to talk about, so it was a bit awkward, the two of us just treading water, staring at each other. "I'm getting tired," she finally said. "I'd better go back to shore. But you can stay out here."

I didn't say anything, just flipped over onto my back and started kicking. She swam right alongside me. Sometimes we'd be on our backs, sometimes we'd roll like otters, onto our sides, our stomachs, back again. There was no hurry, and by the time we got to the shore, Karen seemed calm. She swam in to the shallows, tucked her skirt under her ass and sat on the cool stones, watching me like she was expecting an answer to some question I was pretty sure she'd never asked.

I swam around a bit more but didn't go far, and eventually I worked my way into the shallows and sat beside her, my elbows resting on my drawn-up knees. I kept myself from edging in too close to her, even though of course I wanted to. Her dress was wet and clinging to her in lots of interesting places, and it would have felt totally natural to explore those places a little. And, okay, I admit it, I snuck a few peeks. But I kept my hands to myself, even though I wasn't really sure why. I mean, Karen was different from other girls I'd known, sure, but that wasn't really what was holding me back. It was more like *I* was different, or at least like I wanted to be.

So I didn't make any of the moves I knew so well. Instead I said, "Must be lots to do in the city. This is probably boring, eh?"

"No. It's not boring. It's really nice." She seemed to mean it, and I took her at her word. I checked in a few times through the day, making sure she wasn't ready to leave, but she always seemed totally content to stay there. We just hung out, swimming and lying in the sun and talking about stupid stuff. I got a lot better at knowing when she was about to get uncomfortable, and she started to loosen up a little, like she was trusting me to not push in somewhere that was none of my business.

Finally, though, I looked at my watch and said, "You probably need to get home for dinner?" It wasn't that I wanted to leave, but I didn't want to start creeping her out again.

Karen didn't answer, but I could hear her stomach growl, and we both grinned. I got dressed, and she pulled her sandals on, and we walked slowly back to the truck. I was warm and relaxed from the sun and the swimming, but it was more than just that. I couldn't remember the last time I'd spent a whole afternoon with someone where hockey hadn't been mentioned a single time.

We didn't talk as we drove back to town, but it was a comfortable silence. We were both tired, and there wasn't anything that needed to be said until I had to ask, "Where am I taking you?"

She paused before giving me the address, and I worried that she was back to the old he's-a-psycho thing, but she finally coughed it up and asked, "Do you know where that is?"

"I know the street. You can point out the house when we get there."

When we turned the corner onto her street she said, "It's the yellow brick one with the pillars, halfway down on the right." We got a little closer, and I could feel her tensing up as she said, "The one with all the people out front."

I recognized a few of the faces and had a sudden urge to keep driving. We could just keep going, maybe circle around and go back to the lake. We could live on wild strawberries and fish, and maybe sleep in the truck, or build a shack on the beach...

But Karen already thought I was psycho; I didn't need to give her further evidence. So I pulled up to the curb and watched as everyone turned to look at us. I saw the recognition, and forced myself to stare straight ahead. I didn't know what Karen was doing, living with these people, but I knew that at least one of them would really prefer that I drop dead.

I didn't think I'd mention that to Karen.

Chapter Five

- *KAREN* -

When we pulled up to the curb, the heads of the perfect family all swiveled in our direction. The grandperfects were there, dressed as if they'd been playing golf, and as I watched, Matt pulled a set of clubs out of the back of their SUV. Of course—the twins had been bonding with Grandma and Grandpa. How sweet.

I should clarify that these were Natalie's parents, not my father's, and after that I probably don't have to go into a lot of detail about their expressions as they looked over and saw the evidence of their daughter's humiliation sitting there in a pickup truck. Honestly, it was a disgrace that I was even allowed to walk around and be seen with civilized human beings.

"You live here?" Tyler asked. "With the Beacons?"

I really wasn't up to explaining. "Shining Beacons of

hope," I said earnestly. "We can only pray that they'll be able to reach a sinner like me." I opened my door and slid out before he could say anything more. My dress was still a bit damp and it stuck to the seat and dragged out behind me; I think my lack of mortification about that makes it clear just how awkward the situation already was. Flashing my ass at a cute boy was the least of my worries. "Thanks," I said quickly as I shut the door. "Fun afternoon," I added through the window, and then I turned toward the house. I would have liked to just slink around the back and find my way in through the kitchen door, but one look at the crowd made it clear that wasn't going to fly.

"Hi," I said as calmly as I could manage. I was dimly aware of the truck driving away behind me, and that was a relief, at least. "I'm going to go get changed."

"What the hell happened to you?" Matt asked. I was tempted to reprimand him for using strong language in mixed company, but I was sure his conscience would provide him with punishment enough.

I looked down at myself and shrugged. "Yeah. I'm a mess. So I'll just go get changed."

"What were you doing with Tyler MacDonald?" This time it was Miranda talking. Apparently the twins were the designated spokespeople for the group, and everyone seemed interested in hearing my answer.

"Just hanging out. Swimming." I tried to toss my hair nonchalantly, but it was still a little wet and totally tangled from driving with the windows down, so it just sort of slapped against the side of my head.

"With *Tyler MacDonald*?" she said scornfully. Her eyes were cold as she added, "I hope you used protection."

"Miranda!" Natalie exclaimed, and the grandparents turned to her with round eyes.

"*I'm* not the one who just climbed out of Tyler MacDonald's sex-wagon," Miranda said haughtily. "And honestly… she should use protection. I know it should go without saying, but obviously she wasn't getting a great example at home, if you know what I mean. Maybe she hasn't been living here long enough to unlearn the slut-washing."

I was kind of in shock. Miranda had been cold up to now, but she'd never been vicious. Then I remembered the overheard conversation in the drug store and realized that maybe Miranda had been attacking me all along, but she'd been doing it behind my back. "The example your father's setting, you mean?" I suppose it was sinking to her level, but screw it; I was ready to sink. "'Cause from what I've heard, *he's* the big slut around here. At least my mother wasn't cheating on a pregnant wife when she went slumming."

I saw Natalie's face and felt a little bit guilty, but if she didn't want to hear the truth spoken out loud, she should have kept a muzzle on her daughter. "I'm going to get changed," I said. The grandparents seemed shocked, Natalie looked ill, and both of the twins clearly wanted me dead. Just as I yanked the front door open, I heard a new car pull into the driveway and turned around to see Will's smile fading as he saw the expressions of the gathered crowd. *Yeah. Welcome home, daddy. We sure did miss you.*

I resisted the urge to play my mom's phone message. Instead, I stayed in the shower for longer than was justifiable, then spent quite a while combing through the tangles in my hair and getting dressed. A sundress and a sweatshirt shouldn't take all that long to put on. I even used mascara and lip gloss and thought about investing in more makeup. It might be nice to have some sort of mask between me and the rest of the world.

At least *most* of the rest of the world.

The afternoon with Tyler had been an exception: even though I really wanted him to find me attractive, I didn't want to wear a mask with him. I'd felt like maybe, just maybe, he'd be happier to see me as I actually was.

I spent about thirty seconds thinking about Miranda's wild accusations. Tyler's sex-wagon? Seriously? There had been so many chances for him to be sleazy, or even flirty, but he hadn't taken any of them. Maybe living with her dad had made Miranda unable to see any men without thinking they were sluts.

The knock on my bedroom door wasn't exactly surprising, but I wasn't sure who I would find when I opened it. I definitely wasn't expecting Sara, and the retorts I'd come up with didn't make sense when I was dealing with an innocent fourteen-year-old. Well played, whoever sent her.

"Hi," she said tentatively. "Can I come in?"

I couldn't think of a way to say no, so I stepped aside and she eased past me, stopping awkwardly in the middle of the room. She turned all the way around, then said, "Everything still looks the same. I thought you'd have changed it, maybe. Put up posters or something." She looked at me quickly, then looked away as she said, "If you want to paint, I can help. Mom always hires painters, but I helped paint Becky Robinson's bedroom and it wasn't that hard."

"It's okay. I'm not sure how long I'll be here for, so we should probably just leave it the way your mom likes it."

She frowned and sat down on the corner of my bed.

"You're here for the school year at least, aren't you? I mean, maybe you'll go away to university next fall, but you're here for the year? That's what mom and dad said."

I shrugged. "Hard to be sure."

Sara nodded but didn't say anything. She also didn't get up to leave. I had no idea what I was supposed to be doing or saying, but she was obviously expecting something more. Finally she sighed and flopped dramatically backward, the comforter fluffing up around her outstretched arms. "You don't like us, do you?"

"*You* seem nice," I tried.

"But the rest of the family? And Corrigan Falls? Do you like the town, even?"

"I just got here, Sara. I'm still trying to figure it all out."

"It'll be better once school starts," she said, like she was trying to cheer me up. "You can make friends with people and they'll show you around." Another one of her quick looks, like she wasn't sure how much she wanted to say to me. "I could do that, too, but I guess you probably aren't too interested in hanging out with a kid."

"A kid? I thought you were fourteen?"

"Yeah…"

"Fourteen isn't a kid. You're in high school this year, right?"

"Yeah." She didn't seem too happy about the direction the conversation was taking. Maybe she didn't want to be the one in charge of introducing the pariah around town. Luckily for her, we heard the sounds of someone coming down the basement steps, and we both turned our heads to see my father—*our* father—appear in the doorway.

"Hey, guys," he said. He seemed surprised to see Sara

down there. "Uh…Miranda and Matt are going out for piz-za, but Mom and I" —he caught himself— "Natalie and I… we've got dinner ready."

Sara stood up quickly. "Excellent. I'm starving."

She wasn't the only one, but I wasn't looking forward to spending another strained half-hour at that dining room table, staring at my food and trying to ignore all the secret messages and meaningful looks whizzing around the room. And things only got worse when Will said, "Actually, Sara, the twins thought you might like to go with them."

Sara froze, then turned her head toward Will. "Me *and* Karen?" she said with a meaningful glare. "*All* the kids?"

God, it was sad to see a grown man squirm like a little boy. "Well, no. Natalie and I thought it might be a good time for us to talk to Karen."

"I'll stay here," Sara decided. "Half your kids one place, the other half somewhere else."

I really wanted to hug her. I mean, I wasn't looking forward to having her as an audience for whatever Natalie and Will had planned for me, but I appreciated her efforts to do the right thing. Judging by the expression on his face, Will did not share my sentiments. "But pizza's your favorite. Matt and Miranda picked it just for you."

"They can bring me back a slice," Sara said.

"Sara." A new voice from the doorway, and Natalie frowned as she stepped into the room. "You'll go to din-ner with Matt and Miranda. Your dad and I need to talk to Karen."

"Mom—" Sara started, but Natalie raised an eyebrow and Sara fell silent. It was impressive, really. I wondered if she trained her family with those shock collars for dogs, giving them a zap every time they had a thought of their own. The kid turned to me and apologetically said, "I'll come see you when I get back?"

"If I'm still here," I said sweetly.

She gave me a little frown, glowered at each of her parents in turn, and stalked out of the room.

Natalie smiled brightly. "Chicken enchiladas. They're probably getting a bit cold, but we can heat them if we need to. Let's go!"

She made it sound like we were heading to summer camp, not walking down death row. But I guess death row isn't all that big of a deal, for the guards.

I trudged along behind them, contemplating escape but drawn by the mouth-watering aromas coming from the dining room. I could eat, and pretend to listen, and it'd all be over with soon enough.

We sat in our accustomed seats, Natalie decided the food was hot enough to eat as is, and we dug in. Nobody talked for a while, which was great, but finally Natalie said, "So, Karen. That was a bit of a scene this afternoon."

"Yes, it was." I'd fantasized about playing it this way when I was in the shower, but I couldn't believe I actually had the nerve to do it in real life. "It was quite upsetting for me. I think it's important that I have a stable home environment at this stage of my development, and I'd like to make sure nothing like that happens again. If you can assure me that Miranda's behavior will be under better control, I may be able to accept that. But, otherwise, I think you should seriously consider boarding school. I know it's late in the year, but I'm sure there's still *somewhere* that would accept her."

They both stared at me, and then Will took a long drink

of water.

"That's not an option we're considering," Natalie finally said. "For either of you."

"Me? Why on earth would you consider banishing *me* from this happy family home?"

"Karen," Natalie said with a sigh, "Give it a rest. You and Miranda had a fight. She started it, but you didn't have to join in."

And that was it for the little game. "Your bitch of a daughter called my mother a slut, and you think *I* should have backed down? Seriously?"

"Let's take it easy on the name calling," she replied. "You need to understand that this is a difficult adjustment for all of us, not just for you."

"Then why the hell are we doing it? I mean, there *are* options. If not boarding school, then maybe I should just go back to the city and stay with friends or get an apartment or something. I'm sixteen, not six. This *adjustment* is totally unnecessary, for all of us."

"We're your family," Natalie said firmly. "We should have gotten to know you earlier, but we can't go back in time and change that. What we *can* change is the present and the future. We need to get to know each other and figure out how to get along, and we can't do that if you're living three hours away from the rest of us." She took a sip of her water, then nodded firmly as if she'd re-convinced herself of her own wisdom. "This is an opportunity. There will be challenges, but nothing we can't overcome. We just need to have a clearer set of expectations for everybody."

"Expectations?" I cocked my head at her. "Okay, here's one: if your bitch of a daughter calls my mother a slut again, she can absolutely *expect* me to beat the shit out of her."

"Let's settle down a little," Will started, but he stopped talking when I whirled to face him.

"And maybe you could help me out with another area of expectation. From what I'm hearing, you haven't exactly changed your ways on the cheating front. So, just so we all know: should we *expect* to see any more extra kids rolling into the house, or did you at least learn your lesson about birth control?" It felt good to see his expression change, and the furtive look he sent in Natalie's direction was as clear an admission of guilt as I'd ever seen. I couldn't decide whether to be disgusted by him or kind of satisfied at being right.

"Karen, leave the table, please." Natalie's voice was tightly controlled. "Go to your room and stay there until you're able to have a civil conversation."

I stood up so fast my chair almost fell over. "Sure, fine. Why don't you two let me know when *you're* ready to have a conversation, one that's based on honesty instead of trying to pretend everything's okay. How's that sound?"

I stormed out through the kitchen, but on my way to the stairs I saw the back door and couldn't resist. So I took my chance to escape, letting the door slam behind me as I headed around to the sidewalk in front of the house. I stood there, trying to decide which way to start walking, until I realized that it didn't matter. It didn't matter which direction I chose, because there was no destination in mind. I had absolutely nowhere to go.

A set of headlights appeared at the corner and turned down the street toward me. I had a quick flash of hope, so strong that I actually believed. The lights came closer and I saw that they were on a pickup truck, and I brushed the tears out of my eyes so Tyler wouldn't see them when he pulled over and asked if I needed a ride. I took half a step forward, heading for the curb, and the truck got closer and then it drove right on by, and I saw some middle-aged man in the driver's seat, staring at the road ahead as if I didn't even exist.

I was so stupid. Right after my mother's car crash, I'd go visit her in the hospital and every time I opened the door to her room I'd truly expect her to be sitting up in bed, looking a bit beat up, maybe, but smiling at me and gesturing for me to come over so I could lay my head on her lap and she could comb through my hair with her long, slender fingers. "I'm sorry I scared you," she'd say, and I'd cry but tell her that it wasn't her fault.

Every time I'd walked into her room and seen her still lying there unconscious, I'd felt the same sick twisting in my stomach that I was feeling there on the sidewalk watching the tail lights disappear around the next corner. My mom was gone. Tyler wasn't going to rescue me. I had nowhere to go, and no one who cared. I started walking, but I didn't hurry.

There was absolutely no reason to.

Chapter Six

- *TYLER* -

My billet family was nice enough, but there were only two reasons that anyone allowed an unrelated teenage boy to live in their homes for ten months of the year: they either needed the money, or they were *big* hockey fans. The Cavalis were fans, and it got a bit tiring.

"So how was practice today?" It had been Rob Cavali, the father, who asked, but every head in the room swiveled to wait for my answer. I had it on good authority that the family only had dinner together when they had a hockey player to interrogate; over the summer or when the team was out of town, they grabbed meals whenever it was convenient. But with me there, it was a different story.

"Pretty good," I said. I knew from experience that this wasn't going to be nearly enough for them, so I added, "The rookies are still working really hard, trying to earn their spots. And the rest of the team came back strong and fit."

"So you're going to beat Peterborough, then? On Sunday?" Little Robbie was a true believer, his face glowing like he was having a conversation with God. No pressure, of course. Lots of fun to come home to this house after we lost a game.

"Sunday's just an exhibition," Robbie's sister Christina said with all the scorn she could muster. "It's for trying out new players, not *winning*." Christina was thirteen and starting to be a bit of a nuisance, her interest shifting from the hockey itself to the guys underneath the uniforms. If the Cavalis kept billeting players after she got her braces off, they'd be asking for trouble.

The rest of the meal, as usual, was an interrogation, and I wasn't sorry to escape to my room with the excuse that I had to watch game films. I turned on my laptop and hit "play", but then I flopped down on the bed and stared up at the ceiling. I knew it was coming, so I just waited for it, and sure enough, my cell phone played the distinctive tone that always made me want to smash it against the wall.

I picked the phone up and said, "Hey, Dad."

"Tyler. You're at home, right? Your truck's here."

It was great, being stalked by my own father. "Yeah, I'm at home."

"Come outside. I want to talk to you."

Of course he did. I hung up and swung my legs over the side of the bed, then just sat there for a few seconds before heaving myself to my feet and heading for the door. There was no point in delaying the inevitable.

I got outside and looked around for my dad's beat up Toyota but didn't see it. That was when a bulky-looking SUV flashed its lights at me and I peered through the darkness to see my father sitting behind the wheel.

I crossed the street and cautiously eased into the passenger seat, and we pulled out into the street. I sniffed at the new car smell and ran my hands over the leather seats, just waiting. My dad liked to be driving when we had these conversations; it gave him an excuse to not look at his disappointment of a son.

"Your coach is living in the past," he said firmly. "First off, you don't need that much endurance to play hockey; it's a game of sprints, not a marathon. Running is just a way to get injured, with no payoff. And second, if you *are* going to run, you need to do it somewhere public. The treadmill would be best and safest, but if you need to be outside you should run around the parking lot at the arena, or something. Somewhere people can see how hard you're working."

"Coach said not to change my training." I sounded like a little kid, almost whining, and I hated it.

"Me and Brett say differently." There was something in the way he said my agent's name that made the back of my neck itch.

"Where's the Toyota, Dad? Where'd you get this from?"

He shook his head impatiently. "The Toyota's dead. This is a loaner."

"Loaned from who?" My dad was an unemployed drywaller. He didn't have friends who had brand-new SUVs lying around waiting to be borrowed.

"From Brett. From the guy who's actually looking out for you and your family."

"He loaned you an SUV?"

"Loaned, leased…whatever. He saw that I was driving a

piece of shit, and he did something about it."

I tried not to react. It was none of my business, and there was nothing I could do about it, anyway. But I could practically hear one more chain wrapping around me and being locked tight, attaching me to an agent, a career, a life…

"He said he'd asked you about wheels, and you said you were all set." My dad still didn't look at me, but I could see him snarling in disgust. "Why the hell wouldn't you go for an upgrade?"

"There's nothing wrong with my truck."

"There's plenty wrong with that truck."

"I only have one parking spot."

"Jesus, Tyler, you'd throw out the goddamn truck! Do you really think you're going to be cruising around in that piece of crap when you're in the NHL?"

There was no point in having the fight. I'd said it all before. What if I wasn't good enough to *make* the NHL? That question just showed that I was weak-willed and not devoted enough to my game. What if I was good enough but got injured? I was being a pessimist, talking like an old man. Of course I wasn't going to get injured. There was one question I'd never dared to ask, though: What if I didn't *want* to play in the NHL?

"You're a strange kid, Tyler." He sounded defeated, as if he'd made every effort to understand my twisted mind but just couldn't manage it. "But it makes more sense for me to have it, anyway. I have to drive back and forth a lot."

Again, there was an argument that I didn't bother even starting. Because he *didn't* have to drive back and forth. Most parents tried to come by for the big games, or at least came to watch when the team was at an away game near their homes, but there were plenty of guys whose parents hardly ever showed up. My dad was one of the few who made it to every home game and most of the away games; he'd tried to convince the coach to let him ride on the team bus last year, but thankfully that hadn't worked out. It was convenient for my dad that he was unemployed, I guess; there's no way he could have held a job down anyway, and I was pretty sure hockey would always come first with him.

"So it worked out fine," I said. "Everything's good."

"No, it's *not* good. Not when you're wasting your damn energy running around town instead of training." His voice was loud, bouncing back off the windshield right into my face. "I don't want you to do it anymore. No more."

"I can't change my training without the team's approval, dad. You know that." And it was time for the secret weapon. "Nobody's going to want to draft a difficult player. I have to work with the team, do what they say."

"Your coach is an idiot."

"The trainer agrees with him."

"The trainer *works* for him. Brett says we should look into building our own support staff. You need independent advice on this stuff."

"I make two hundred and twenty dollars a week. I don't have money for 'support staff,' and neither do you."

"Brett says he can get you a loan. It'd be like an advance against your future income."

There was no way on Earth that was a good idea. But I had no new arguments to make, and he wouldn't have heard them anyway. "I'll think about it," I said. I wasn't lying. It was hard *not* to think about it all.

"And don't run tomorrow."

The team was doing fitness testing the next day, and the trainer had already told me to come in fresh, so it was easy for me to say, "Okay. I'll take tomorrow off. And I'll talk to the trainer about it."

He'd got what he wanted, so he circled back around and pulled up outside the Cavali house. "This is an important year for you, Tyler. Don't screw it up."

I didn't bother saying good-bye, just jumped out of the SUV and slammed the door behind me. If I'd had my keys in my hand, I think I'd have put a pretty long scratch in his shiny new paint as he drove away, but I was too slow, and he was gone.

I thought about going for a drive myself, but there's times when I see myself doing the same shit my dad does and it freaks me out. I didn't want to be out on the road at the same time as him, both of us circling around, trying to figure out how to make our lives make sense.

No, I didn't want that. So I walked instead, and my body followed the route I took on my morning runs. The Cavalis lived in a nicer neighborhood than my own family, but it still wasn't ritzy or anything. The best part about it was how close to the park it was, and the best thing about the park was how few people ever seemed to use it. When I arrived there that night, there was enough moonlight to show me a big, empty sweep of grass, ending in the forest on the far side. Lots of space for me to just be alone and think about it all, or, even better, space for me to be alone and *not* think, if I could manage it.

I headed for the two wooden benches that sat in the middle of the park, facing each other in the middle of all that space like two ships tied together in the middle of the ocean. I wasn't too impressed when I got close and realized there was someone lying on one of the benches.

I'd never lived in a city, but I'd visited a few and seen homeless people and drunks and whoever sleeping in public. But somehow I wasn't getting that vibe from this person. I stepped a little closer and the body made a startled sound and sat up.

"Karen," I said. It was too dark to see her clearly, but there was something about the way she ran her hands across her face that let me know she'd been crying. Shit. I wasn't much good at being the comforting guy, and this was none of my business. I had my own stuff to worry about, and I'd already messed up once with someone in the Beacon house so I didn't really want to dive into another mess. But still, I took a couple steps forward. "You okay?"

"What are you doing here?"

"Squirrel hunting. They let down their guard at night."

She looked at me for a few breaths as if trying to decide whether to go along with my nonsense, then finally said, "You don't have a gun."

"I use my teeth. Want to help?"

"Do I want to help you hunt squirrels with your teeth? Not tonight, no."

"Some other time, maybe." I sank down carefully onto the other bench, twisting around so I was still more or less looking at her.

"I have seriously never had this many squirrel-conversations with one person before in my whole life."

"Welcome to Corrigan Falls." I guess I probably should have taken the conversation in a more meaningful direction from there. I should have asked her more about why she'd come here, or why she was living with the Beacons. I absolutely should have mentioned that Miranda Beacon hated my guts and probably had a fairly good reason to. Yeah, there were all kinds of responsible things I should have done.

Instead, I swung my feet up on the bench and lay back, looking up at the stars like Karen had been doing before I arrived. I guess what I *should* have done was leave her alone, but something about the tears had made me think she hadn't really *wanted* to be alone. And after running into her, I didn't want it anymore, either. "You watching the stars?" I asked.

"I guess." She didn't sound hostile or anything, just a little sheepish.

"You know anything about them? The constellations or anything?"

"Not really. You?"

"Oh, yeah, I'm pretty much an expert. That one right there, over toward the trees. Big Dipper, obviously."

"Okay, *that* one I knew."

"The one over to its left?" I raised my arm and tried to trace the picture. "Two squares, kind of? That's Rodentus minor, the angry squirrel."

"Oh my god, you're obsessed."

"But don't worry. Runner majoricus is right there to rescue any fair maidens who are attacked."

"Is that how you've built it up in your head? You're a great big hero?" She sounded better now, and I let myself relax a little more.

"I don't know what you're talking about. These are the stars we're looking at. I'm not saying there's any connection to any real life events."

She was quiet for a moment, then lifted her own arm and

pointed. "So, those ones there. Those aren't Driver horrificus and Passenger odiferous?"

And right there, lying on the bench in the summer darkness, it was like I had a weird out of body experience. I knew the logical response, the one that would take me the next step down the path I always took. Attractive, friendly girl, already lying down, under the damn stars...it was too easy, really, but that had never stopped me before. I should say it was actually Driver horrificus and Passenger beauteous, or something. I should build on the fair maiden line I'd dropped a little earlier. Either of those would work.

But it was like there was another me, one looking down at the scene, and that me saw how nice things could be just as they were. It told me I didn't need to push forward, didn't need to race for the goal line. Just this once, I didn't have to be quite so focused on scoring.

So instead of feeding her a line, I smiled up at the stars. "Damn," I said. "That *is* what those ones are. I guess maybe there's some connection after all."

We lay there a while longer, looking up at the stars and trading lies that somehow felt like the truth. And when Karen finally sighed and sat up and said it was late and she had to go back to her real life, I knew she was right. But I really wished the two of us could have stayed in our little make-believe world at least a little longer.

Chapter Seven

- *KAREN* -

Tyler insisted on walking me home, even though I told him I was fine. When we got to the house, he waited on the sidewalk until I was in the backyard. I turned back for one more look at him before I went around the corner of the house, and I froze, torn between knowing I had to go inside and wanting, wanting so bad, to run back to him. I wasn't sure what I'd do when I reached him—it didn't matter, really. Just being with him, being with someone normal and sane and kind, someone funny and sweet who seemed to actually be happy to see me and want to spend time with me. That was all I wanted.

But he couldn't see me hesitating in the shadows, and he turned around and started off toward whatever his real life was, so I was able to make myself be responsible.

All the lights in the house were off, so I found the hide-akey in the back yard. When I got to the kitchen door, though, it was unlocked, and when I stepped inside Will was sitting at the table, no light except for what was filtering in from the hall. He'd been waiting for me. He asked, "You're okay?" in a quiet voice.

I nodded mutely, and he stood up. "Okay. Go to bed. We'll talk tomorrow."

That was all. He turned and headed for his staircase; I turned and headed for mine. If I hadn't been so tired I probably would have been worried about the next day's conversation, but as it was, I played my mom's message a couple times, then fell asleep fast and easy.

I woke up the next morning with the dawn, and it took me two blinks to realize where I was. There was the familiar weight of reality, the renewed realization of why I was there and what I had lost. When I was asleep, I was still in my bed in Toronto, and my mother was still safely sleeping in the room next door. Every time I woke up, I lost her again, and it took me a while to adjust.

Then I rolled out of bed and reached for my running clothes. I had to keep moving, keep distracting myself. And I was over my pathetic need to be rescued, at least temporarily, but that didn't mean I couldn't look forward to seeing Tyler.

There was no sign of him when I got to the park, but that wasn't a big deal. It wasn't like we'd set a time, or anything. Thinking back, there hadn't even been a "see you tomorrow morning". Just a quiet "good night" on the sidewalk.

I stretched for maybe a little longer than usual, definitely long enough for him to have completed a lap of the path through the forest, so I knew he wasn't there yet. No big deal. Maybe he was just late. I started jogging and tried to get into my rhythm. Usually, I could totally drown out my thoughts with a sort of mental chant, thinking along with the sound of my feet hitting the path, the measured pace of my breathing. *In, thud thud, out, thud thud, in, thud thud…* It wasn't exactly exciting, but it was great to turn my brain off for a while. But that day, I kept being distracted. I thought I saw him about a dozen times, either in front of me or behind, just out of sight, and in a move of rare brilliance I actually reversed the direction that we both normally ran so I'd be sure I'd go past him if he was there, instead of both of us running around at the same pace on opposite sides of the circuit.

I kept at it for way longer than usual, long enough that the sun was getting hot and my legs were starting to feel like wobbly blades of grass, but Tyler didn't appear.

It wasn't a big deal. It was stupid to feel disappointed. Everything was fine, and it was great that I'd gotten such a good workout. I stretched out on the benches in the grassy area of the park and then walked home, and I did *not* look over my shoulder a bunch of times to check in case he'd just been really late.

Will's car was gone by the time I got back which was an excellent side effect of the extra-long workout, but the rest of the family seemed to be awake, which was a definite drawback. I tried to sneak in, but Natalie was waiting for me in the kitchen. I needed to check and see if any of the basement windows opened—maybe I could turn one of them into my own entrance/exit route.

"Karen," Natalie said firmly. "Come in here for a minute, please."

"I'm totally sweaty and gross. I'll just shower, and then—"

"Now, please. It won't take long." There was something in her tone that made me obey, and I realized she didn't need to use shock collars on her kids; she was just an authoritative person.

Still, I might do what she said, but I didn't have to do it nicely. So I slumped against the fridge, letting my sweaty body steam up the stainless steel, and raised an eyebrow at her. *I'm waiting*, my body language said. *This had better be good.*

Natalie kept her eyes on me as she stepped out into the front hall and called up the stairs. "Miranda? Come down here, please."

Natalie returned to the kitchen, and a moment later Miranda appeared, looking cautious. When she saw me, her expression faded to sullen. Probably a good mirror of my own face.

"Ladies," Natalie said. "I've tried to speak to both of you individually, and I haven't had much luck. So let's try this as a group."

We both just stared at her. She shook her head and said, "That little display yesterday was absolutely unacceptable. I do *not* want a repeat of it, under any circumstances. Is that clear?"

I snorted. "If you can get your daughter to keep her mouth shut, there shouldn't be a problem."

"Oh my God!" Miranda's eyes were wide with faked outrage. "Mom, she's running around with *Tyler MacDonald*. I told you yesterday, she needs to be kept on a leash or something. Honestly, some of the things she could catch from him? I don't think she should be allowed to use the same toilet seats as us, is all I'm saying."

"Both of you, stop it!" Natalie stared at us like we were rabid wolverines who'd somehow fought our way into her spotless kitchen. "Karen, I want you *both* to keep your mouths shut, and Miranda, if you want Karen to make different friends, maybe you should introduce her to some of *yours*."

Miranda was in the middle of making a disgusted face, but I beat her to the punch. "No, thanks. From what I've seen of them, I'm really not interested."

"What you've seen of them?" Miranda snarled. "You haven't seen them at all. Since you got here, I've been too embarrassed to let anyone come over!"

"You think I heard about your dad's whoring from Tyler? Trust me, we talk about stuff *way* more interesting than your pathetic family. No, it was your so-called friends who were talking about it." And since this whole showdown had been Natalie's stupid idea, I added, "From what they say, though, I could have heard it anywhere, because apparently the whole *town* knows he's a complete slut."

"You are a total *bitch*!" Miranda screamed. "You're ruining everything. Mom, this is my last year before university, and she's going to *ruin* it." She was crying now, her face twisted up and blotchy, and I almost felt sorry for her. But not quite.

I had my mouth open for the next attack when Natalie said, "Enough!" She stepped between the two of us and said, "Sit down. Both of you." Neither of us moved, and Natalie growled, "Miranda..." and pointed at one of the kitchen chairs. There was a tense moment, but finally Miranda moved, and Natalie turned toward me. "Karen," she said more calmly, and gestured to a chair on the far side of the table.

I figured I could always just stand up again if I had to, so I moved, and Natalie sank tiredly into her own chair between the two of us. "No more," she finally said. "I don't want to hear the words 'bitch' or 'slut' or 'whore' one more time in this house. Not from either one of you, not directed at each other or anybody else."

"What about the *idea* of slut?" I asked. It probably sounded petty, but I was pretty sure I had a point. "Like the stuff she keeps saying about Tyler?" I wasn't sticking up for his honor; I just wanted to see her face.

Natalie nodded slowly. "I think his name should probably be off-limits as well." She shook her head at Miranda. "Honestly, I've never heard you have a problem with him before. Where did all this come from?"

"From me finding out what a whore he is," Miranda said.

"Uh, consequences," I sing-songed. "She used a forbidden word. She obviously needs a consequence in order to understand that you're serious."

"You want consequences?" Natalie rolled her head toward me, looking absolutely disgusted. "Fine. For both of you." She looked back at Miranda. "The garage is a mess. Today, *both of you* will be cleaning it out. I want it totally emptied, then swept down and hosed out." She looked at each of us in turn, and I began to understand the true horror of what she was saying. "I'll have Matt and Sara sort through their things, and Will is planning to be home at lunch, so he can go through his stuff as well. Whatever they decide to keep, you two will find a home for. Whatever they decide to throw out, you will load up and take to the dump or to Goodwill. Neither one of you will leave this house until that job is finished."

"Wait a second," I said. "Why the hell am I clearing out all *your* junk? I just moved here." I refused to mention the pain of dealing with my mother's things at the apartment, because there was no way on earth I was going to cry in front of either of these two. But I really felt like I'd done enough sorting of belongings for a while.

"You're doing it because you need to learn to get along with your sister, and maybe working on a shared task will help with that."

"That's bullshit. She's only my *half*-sister, and spending a whole day trapped with her is only going to make it *more* clear what a psycho-bitch she is!"

"And *now* you're doing it as a consequence for using one of the forbidden words," Natalie said with a coldly charming smile. "You can have half an hour to shower and have breakfast, but I want both of you in the garage by nine o'clock, ready to work."

"Mom, Claire and Lisa and I are going to the movies this afternoon. We made plans!" Miranda sounded like she might start crying again.

"Well, then, you'd better work fast." Natalie shook her head. "I don't think you're going to make it, to be honest, but...maybe. You can try, at least." Damn, this was a new side to the woman—who knew she had a sadistic streak? I was almost ready to appreciate her when she turned to me and said, "Are you thinking that there's no point getting showered, because the job is going to be so dirty? Or are you just wasting valuable time?"

I stared at her for as long as I could, but there was no way she was going to back down. So I forced my face into a smile just as artificial as all of hers and said, "Super. I'm sure this will work. No problem." Another smile to make it clear I was being sarcastic, and then I stomped downstairs to get cleaned up.

By the time I'd eaten and gone to the garage, Miranda was already hard at work. It was still before nine, so I guess she was just being a martyr. I flopped down on the steps leading to the house and watched her for a while.

"Are you going to *help*?" she finally asked.

"I don't know. *I* don't have anywhere to be this afternoon. I was thinking about taking it slow."

She glared at me, then slowly, deliberately reached into her pocket and pulled out her phone. She hit the screen a few times and then raised it to her ear. "Hi," she said. "I'm just calling because I can't make it this afternoon. Yeah, there's a family thing. That girl who's staying with us? Yeah. It's her fault. So, anyway, I'm not going to make it." She nudged a big canvas bag full of hockey gear with her foot, then sank gracefully down onto it and smiled at me. "Yeah, she's still living here. You should see her. We're supposed to be cleaning out the garage, and she's wearing a *dress*. I honestly don't know if she even owns a pair of jeans."

Miranda was loving this, and I was kind of stuck. I couldn't leave without it looking like I was running away, and if I got up and started moving things, she'd have won. So I just sat there and stared out the garage door as she kept talking. "Yeah, it's like she thinks she's better than us. 'Oooh, I'm from the city, and I wear dresses all the time.' And meanwhile, she's, like, a pathetic little rat-creature, with her pointy face and her nasty brown hair." She giggled, "No, *you* have *nice* brown hair. It's a real color! Hers is just dirty dishwater."

Where the hell was Natalie? Shouldn't she be coming out to check on us? She could hear her daughter being a mega-bitch, and then she'd understand what I was dealing with. But I didn't need to be rescued, I reminded myself.

I lurched to my feet and wandered over to the deep shelves that lined Miranda's side of the garage. I shuffled around a little, and I knew she was watching me, just waiting to see me pick up a box of something and move it outside. I picked something up, all right, and I heaved the bag up onto my shoulder and started toward the door. But when I got as far as Miranda, I shifted my grip on the bag and tipped it over, open end down, and let the gritty, dusty birdseed fall on her snarky little head.

It was a big bag and the whole top had been cut open so it didn't pour so much as just empty itself all over her. She shrieked, I laughed, and then she was surging upward, her arms wrapping around my waist as she knocked me over backward onto the hard concrete floor. She landed on top of me and I skidded a bit, feeling the skin on my elbows tearing. Then she had both of her hands wrapped in my hair, "You bitch!" she screamed. "Why did you have to come here? Why!" She tried to bang my head on the floor but she wasn't putting a lot of conviction into it; I kept my neck muscles tense and she barely moved me at all. "I hate you!"

Then Natalie was there, her arm wrapped around Miranda's shoulders as she pulled her backward. "Get off her, Miranda!"

Apparently Miranda was done fighting because she let her mother pull her away from me, and when Natalie let go of her she stalked off to a corner of the garage and just stood there, trembling and crying like *she* was the one who'd almost gotten her head beaten against a concrete floor.

"Psycho!" I said loudly, and I sat up and tried to bend my arms. I sucked in a hissing breath and stopped trying. Instead I just sat there like some sort of demented bird with my wings stretched out to the side and waited to see what happened next.

"Damn it," Natalie said. She crouched down beside me, gently lifting and twisting my arms to see first one elbow and then the other. "These are nasty." She frowned at me. "Do you want me to clean them up, or do you want to go to a doctor?"

"A doctor? They're not that serious, are they?" I tried to twist my arm around to get a better view, but all I saw was a red blur.

"I don't know. They might scar, I guess…" She looked at me as if trying to make a decision, then said, "Miranda, get a clean towel from the laundry room. Get two." She patted my shoulder. "I'll call Doctor Huddleby. He's a friend of the family, and he's very good about getting us in without an appointment." She looked over her shoulder and spoke more sharply. "Miranda! Let's go! Get some towels." She pulled out her phone and started looking for the number, and Miranda kicked herself into gear and started toward the house. "And get my purse," Natalie called after her. Then she turned to me and shook her head. "This can't continue," she said as if it were the most obvious thing in the world. "You two need to figure this out."

"She's psycho," I told her. "Seriously, you should get the doctor to check *her* out."

"Stop it, Karen." Then her smile returned as she spoke

into the phone. "Wendy, hi! It's Natalie Beacon. I'm sorry to bother you, but I'm hoping you can help us out. We've got a teenage girl with some bad scrapes on her arms… I just wanted to get them checked and properly cleaned out, if you could fit us in." Her smile got a little tighter. "No, not Miranda. It's my stepdaughter, Karen. Yes, she's just come to live with us." She looked away from me, out the open garage doors as if she, too, was wishing she could just run away and leave all this behind, but she managed to say, "Yes, of course, it *is* wonderful. There's some adjusting to do, but you're right. It's wonderful." She looked back at me as if she wanted to collect her reward for such a compelling performance, but I just raised my eyebrows.

Yeah, it was wonderful. So wonderful I was bleeding all over her garage floors. If things got any more perfect, I might not be able to survive.

Chapter Eight

- *TYLER* -

"Looking good," the team nutritionist said with a smile, "but I'd like a few more pounds of fat on you, if you can manage it. You're too lean right now… Are you trying to impress the girls with your six-pack?"

"I'm eating all I can. There's only so many hours in the day, and I spend most of them either on the ice or chewing." I didn't want to sound defensive; the nutritionist was there to help. But, damn, it was getting old, not being able to do anything right.

"Let's add a shake," she said easily. "Mostly protein, with a bit of fat. Mix it up and drink it right before bed."

"I already have one in the morning…"

"Then I won't bother giving you instructions on how to mix it." She smiled again. "Seriously, a bit more fat would be good for you. Your growth has slowed down, but I expect you'll end up with another inch or two—"

"He'd better end up with more than that," my dad inter- jected from behind me. "He's barely six-one, now. I'm hop- ing for six-four or so." There wasn't much for anyone to say in response to that little bit of delusion, so he continued, ig- noring me and directing his attention toward the nutrition- ist. "So he'll eat an extra shake. What else? He runs in the mornings; is that burning too many calories?"

After two years, the nutritionist was used to my dad. "We generally prefer to increase food intake rather than decrease exercise," she said smoothly. "The shakes should work. He's not at a dangerous level, just not optimal."

"He needs more muscle, too," my dad insisted, "not just fat. He's too damned small."

"You can talk to the trainers about building muscle," she said calmly. "But I think they're already aware of the issue. And I don't think they consider him too small. As you said, he's six-one, and his weight is good for that height."

My dad didn't look convinced, but he let her go on to talk to the next player. Then he stared at me and said, "You're too damned small."

"I can't make myself grow, Dad."

"Not taller. But you can get bigger. You just need to work harder."

"I'm working hard. The trainers are happy—"

"*I'm* not happy," he barked, and heads swiveled to stare at us. He was already the only parent in the room, having pushed his way in halfway through the testing. He didn't pay any attention to anyone else, though, just shook his head at me with an expression of disgust on his face. "You need to get serious about this, boy." He frowned at me, then jerked his head toward the exit as if he'd made an important decision. "Come here. I want to talk to you."

I didn't bother to point out that he already *was* talking to me. I held up my hand to the coach, fingers outstretched, asking for five minutes, and he nodded reluctantly. I knew he was just hoping to get rid of my father.

We made our way out to the parking lot where my dad leaned against his SUV and said, "I want you to start taking supplements."

"I already take supplements," I said cautiously. "Vitamins, and the protein shakes, and—"

"Not that kind," he said impatiently.

I stared at him and let the idea sink into my brain. "You want me to take *steroids*? Is that what you're saying?" He just stared at me. "Jesus, dad, that's insane! They test us, you know. Random testing. They suspend players. And you know that steroids stunt growth, right? You want me to grow more, you shouldn't be pushing that shit at me."

"Bullshit." His voice was clipped. "I've talked to some people, and there's ways around all that. You can't think nobody else is doing it. Don't even pretend that some of your teammates in there aren't on the juice…"

"Yeah, some of them are," I admitted reluctantly. "The *desperate* ones."

"Well maybe it's time you got a little more *desperate*. You're not big enough, you're not fast enough, you're definitely not working hard enough… You need to pick it up, boy."

It was strange how *I* wasn't allowed to suggest that maybe I didn't have the size for the NHL, but it was fine for him to do it. And the steroids were just a new wrinkle in a fabric that was already crumpled up in a dirty ball. "I'll work harder," I said. "I can add another few reps to my weight training, maybe."

"You could stop running," he said firmly.

I had no idea why I was hanging on to the running as tightly as I was. Partly for Karen, I guess—I was looking forward to seeing her again and wasn't sure where else we'd meet up. But also for me. I liked the way I felt when I was running. I wasn't in a race, wasn't trying to beat a time… I was just running, covering ground because I could.

I knew what my dad expected; he expected me to do the same thing I always had. I'd argue at first, but he'd keep at me, and eventually I'd give in. He didn't care about the running itself, he just wanted to be sure he was still in charge. It was driving him crazy that I hadn't caved yet, and I knew he was just going to keep up the pressure until I did.

But I thought about Karen, her body strong and quick as it darted through the forest, and I thought about myself and how good it felt to do something just for me, and I said, "I'll drink the shakes. The nutritionist said more calories, not less exercise."

My dad shook his head in disgust. "I am about out of patience with this shit, Tyler."

I didn't really know what to say to that.

"I'm going to ask around. See if I can get some samples or something."

"Of steroids?" I shook my head. "Dad, seriously, they test us all the time. You think the scouts are going to want someone who's been busted for juicing?"

"No steroids?" He stepped in closer, right into my space, and said, "Then you're done running outside. You want to run, you do sprints and intervals on the goddamn treadmill, you don't go for a jog in the goddamn woods. You're acting like a little kid. This is your *job*, Tyler. It's your *life*, a chance to go somewhere and do something."

"Yeah, it's *my* life," I responded. I understood the steroids, now—he wasn't actually expecting me to take them, just using them as a threat to get me to knuckle under. "I have to get back in there—the coach gave me five minutes, and I don't want him to think I'm taking advantage."

I started for the building. I heard him coming up behind me, and I lengthened my stride. "The running is *over*, Tyler. As of now. You hear me?"

Yeah, I heard him. And I knew there was no point in arguing. But I didn't think I was going to listen to him.

Chapter Nine

- *Karen* -

The doctor gave me painkillers, and I was able to pretend that I was so doped up on them that I couldn't talk. I lay on my bed with my arms bandaged up and stretched out to the sides like I was about to make a crooked snow angel, and I stared at the ceiling. The scratches on my arms stretched from the top of my elbow to halfway down my forearm, and once they scabbed up, it'd hurt like hell to change the angle my elbows were set at. The doctor had suggested keeping them almost straight, just bent a little, until they scabbed, so I was trying to do that, even if I looked like an idiot. And even with all of that to worry about, I still had a good chunk of my brain that was wondering about Tyler and why he hadn't been in the park that morning, and whether I'd somehow scared him off.

I dozed off at some point, and when I woke up Sara was

sitting cross-legged on the floor, reading a paperback.

"Hey," I said groggily.

She smiled up at me. "Hi. You were asleep, but I wanted to be here in case you needed anything."

I knew I should stay strong, but I was drugged, and hurt, and, damn it, the kid was really sweet. So my words were as gruff as I could make them, but my tone was way gentler than I'd intended when I said, "I'm fine."

"Do your arms hurt?"

"Not right now, no. I think they might if I tried to move them."

She beamed. "That's why I'm here! So you don't have to. I already asked Mom, and she said it was okay to bring the TV in here from the rec room, if you want. We'd have to keep it by the door, I think, because all the hookups are in the other room, but still…we can if you want."

"Is she trying to keep me out of the rec room? In case Miranda goes in there?"

Sara's eyes widened. "No! It was my idea. I just thought you might be more comfortable in here. But you're not in jail. I don't think you're even grounded…but I don't really know about all that."

What the hell would *I* be grounded for? I was the victim here. "Where's Miranda?"

"Working on the garage," Sara said. "Mom said she had to do half, and you could do the rest when your arms healed, but Miranda said there was no way to just half do it because she had to take *everything* out to get it organized right, so Mom said fine, she should do the whole thing. I helped her for a bit, and so did Matt, but she was being so crabby we both quit." Sara stopped talking just long enough to take a deep breath, then said, "She's not normally like this. She's just…" She shook her head. "She's having trouble adjusting, Mom says. But I think there's something more."

"Look, Sara…" It was surprisingly difficult to sit up without changing the angle at which my elbows were bent, but I managed it. Abs of steel. "I appreciate it that you're trying to make me feel welcome. And I know you love your sister. But she doesn't like me, and I don't like her. I don't care what she's upset about, I just want her to shut up and leave me alone. You know?"

"Yeah, but you guys are *both* nice, really. Right? You could get along if you would just stop being so…" She stopped talking when she saw my expression and grinned nervously before making her face serious again. "*Both* of you," she said in a quiet, firm voice that reminded me of her mother. "You're *both* 'having trouble adjusting,' and you're *both* mad about stuff, and it's making *both* of you say stupid, mean things." She checked over her shoulder and then leaned in. "Did you seriously pour a bag of birdseed on her head?"

"She started it!"

"And who would *she* say started it?"

I flopped melodramatically back onto the bed. "Oh my god, you're like a tiny guidance counselor. Leave me alone."

She giggled. "Mom's trying to help, too," she added. "It'd be…" she stopped, then rolled onto her knees and crouched there at the side of the bed like she was getting ready to say her prayers. "It'd be good if you could stop talking about… you know. About Daddy. It's just mean things people say; it's not true. But it still hurts her to hear it."

I wasn't sure how to respond to that. I was walking,

breathing evidence that he'd fooled around on his wife at least once. And if he'd done it once, why wouldn't I believe that he'd done it again? But Sara was just a kid, and she loved her father and wanted to believe the best about him. "I'll try," I finally said. "Hey, if you hook me up with some other stuff that will bug Miranda, I can focus on using that, and leave the cheating out of it."

"Or you could focus on being *nice* to her," Sara said firmly. "That might work."

"I thought you said you were here to *help* me?"

"With watching TV, or holding a book for you or something. Not with finding better ways to be mean!"

"Fine. Let's watch TV."

"Do you want me to bring it in here?"

I really did. But I knew the answer she was hoping for. "No. Let's go out to the rec room. I shouldn't hide in a cave, right?"

She beamed at me. "Right."

So we staggered out to the big leather couches in the rec room, flopped down, and watched TV all afternoon. It was kind of fun, actually. When Natalie came to the top of the stairs and peered down at us, her expression was cautious, but not angry. "Dinner in five minutes, you two."

"Thanks, Mom," Sara chirped. She turned to me. "Can you wash your hands by yourself?"

"Yes. But I have to pee, first. Are you ready to help me with that?"

She made a face, but then said, "You're sure you can't do it yourself?"

I laughed and wanted to tweak her ponytail. "No, I can. Don't worry about it."

"Yell if you get stuck," she said kindly, and scampered off upstairs.

Dinner was about as tense as you'd expect, and of course Natalie insisted that Miranda and I have a talk with her and Will afterward. But honestly, what was there for anyone to say? I bitched some, and Miranda bitched and then cried, Will looked completely out of his depth, and even Natalie seemed exhausted by it all. She ended by saying that she was going to set up family counseling, and all of us, even Will, stared at her, hoping she was joking.

"In the meantime," she said, ignoring our reactions, "you are both on *very* short leashes. There will be no more violence. There will be no more insults. Until you can be-have yourselves, I recommend no more interaction; just stay away from each other for a while. School starts on Tuesday, and hopefully things will settle down when you've got more to occupy your time. I expect the counselor can help us all find more appropriate ways to express ourselves." Now she turned to look at me. Her face was gentle, but she was still way over the line when she said, "Hopefully the counselor can help you deal with your terrible loss. We know you've been through a lot, and we're absolutely ready to give you space *or* support you, or whatever you need. We just hope you can get a little better at letting us know how to help."

If my gaze produced heat, the encyclopedias I was staring at would have been ablaze by the end of her little speech. I kept my eyes pointed in that direction for as long as possible, then flicked a quick look toward her as I said, "Space? That's an option? Excellent. I choose it. Give me some space."

I expected she was disappointed, but I couldn't really

confirm that without looking away from the bookshelf again, which I wasn't going to do. It wasn't like her reaction mattered, anyway. This was about me, not about her.

"Okay," she finally said. "We're here if you need us. And I think Will wanted to talk to you for a while, too." She looked meaningfully in his direction, and he stood up obediently. "Miranda, you stick around, please," she added when her daughter tried to get out of her chair again. Then they all stared at me until I stood up and followed Will out of the room.

I kind of wanted to laugh. We both had to have parental heart-to-hearts, but Miranda was stuck with Natalie and I got Will. He'd be easy. I should probably just ask him about golf and sit back until the requisite time was up. No need for soul-searching here. But I was kind of curious, so I didn't say anything. I just stood there in the hallway with my arms hanging at weird angles, and I waited. This was my father. What the hell did he think he had to say about my life?

Chapter Ten

- TYLER -

I got the phone call that night after dinner. I had to hand it to my dad; he wasn't missing a trick.

"We're so proud of you," my mom said. "And, sweetie, I know it's a lot of pressure, but you need to do the smart thing, right? I mean, it's not just the money. That would help, obviously. Of course we'd love to be able to send your brother and sister to university. Or if Travis wants to play hockey, it'd be great if we could get him the best coaching, send him to all the camps…all the things you had to get by without. Of course that would all be wonderful." I could picture her, sitting there in our tiny kitchen, tired after a long day at the school, where she worked as an educational assistant, looking after other people's kids so she could put food on the table for her own. "But it's not just the money, sweetie. You're a role model. For your brother, for other hockey players, for the whole town. You're showing them that if they work hard their dreams *can* come true."

It felt more like I was showing them that if they worked hard their *dad's* dreams might come true, but that probably wasn't fair. It wasn't like I didn't love the game. Wasn't like I didn't *want* to play at the highest level I could.

"I'm working hard," I said. It sounded sort of defensive.

"Of course you are. But, sweetie, are you working *smart*? Your dad's worried about that. He thinks maybe you aren't taking the best advice from people. I know your coach has an excellent name in the OHL, but your agent has just as good of a name in the NHL. Your coach knows how things are done where you are now, but your agent knows how things are done where you want to be."

"I can't get where I want to be if I don't do well where I am now. And if I want to do well, I have to listen to my coach."

"But this running thing…your coach isn't the one who wants you to do that, is he?"

I couldn't do it. I couldn't have the argument again, couldn't defend myself against requests that seemed totally reasonable to the people making them. *Why does he want to run?* they must be asking themselves. *Why is it such a big deal?* And I didn't know how to answer their unasked questions because I didn't really understand any of it myself.

By the time I got off the phone, I was softened up, just like I usually was after talking to my mom. I knew she'd be calling my dad and telling him she'd done her part, and I didn't want to talk to him until I'd gotten my armor back in place, so I left my phone in my bedroom and headed downstairs. The Cavalis were sitting around on their front porch and invited me to join them, but I knew exactly what they'd want to talk about and I couldn't handle another hockey conversation right then. "I'm meeting somebody," I said, holding up my car keys as if they were some sort of evidence.

Mr. Cavali clapped me on the shoulder. "Enjoy," he said with a little bit of a leer. Even knowing he was jumping to the wrong conclusion, it was still pretty gross thinking of him as someone who was aware of my sex life and thought he had the right to make any sort of comment on it. But that was just one more way that my life wasn't really my own. It was like when I'd signed on to play hockey in Corrigan Falls, I'd signed away any right to privacy or to make my own decisions about much of anything.

I knew how much sympathy I'd get from any of the thousands of guys around the province playing their hearts out and still not making it to the OHL. I was lucky. I couldn't deny it. So that just gave me one more thing to feel bad about. I wasn't big or strong or fast enough, I wasn't working hard enough, I wasn't focused enough, I wasn't thinking about my family enough, and I wasn't even grateful enough.

I wanted to stop thinking about it. And that was when I realized why I was hanging on so hard to my morning runs. They let me turn my brain off. For that hour or so of my day, I wasn't a hockey player, just a guy running through the forest. When Karen had first appeared, I'd actually thought maybe she was there for me, another hockey fan looking for some personal contact, but then I saw the way she ran, the efficient, ground-covering stride, the intense look on her face. Karen was running for reasons of her own, reasons that didn't have a damn thing to do with chasing down some self-centered hockey player.

Toby Cooper, the team's alternate captain, had a girl-friend who was always totally jacked in to what was going on around town, and I'd talked to her after training that afternoon. She'd told me why Karen was in town, and how she was connected to the Beacons, and knowing that had helped me understand things. Karen wasn't impressed with my shit because she had her own stuff going on, stuff more serious than anything I'd ever had to deal with. And even with all that, she was still fighting, trying to find her place and be herself and make up stupid stories about imaginary constellations.

I smiled as I headed for the truck. When I'd left the house, I'd just been trying to get away from my phone, but now I knew where I wanted to go and who I wanted to see. It wasn't smart, but I didn't seem to care. Being with Karen made me feel good, and that was what I needed right then. I just hoped she'd be okay with me showing up.

Chapter Eleven

- *KAREN* -

Will stopped walking in the middle of the kitchen and turned to smile at me. He was in his early forties but still trim and boyishly handsome, and I knew that he expected me to find him charming. He'd been expecting that since I first met him a week and a half ago, and he didn't seem to be realizing how totally unimpressed I was with the whole show.

"TV?" I asked. "We can tell Natalie that we talked."

He looked tempted but shook his head instead. "I thought maybe we could go for a run, if your arms will let you. You like running, right?"

Okay, points for trying to bond over an activity that *I* enjoyed instead of making me go golfing with him or something, but still, "I ran this morning."

"Maybe just a walk, then. You can show me the route you take, and maybe tomorrow I can run with you."

I was still hoping Tyler would be at the park the next day; there was no way I wanted Will there, too. "I go pretty hard. If you're just starting out, you'd get left behind." But maybe I didn't need to be quite so indirect. "Look, Will. I'll try to cool it with Miranda, okay? I will absolutely not start anything, and if she pushes I will make a good effort to not push back. So we're fine. We don't need to do bonding activities. We don't need to have a big talk."

"And you'll go to the counselor? And make a good effort there, too?" He ran both his hands through his dense blond hair and then locked his fingers together behind his neck. For a second I saw behind the charm, and he looked just as bewildered by the latest twist in his life as I was. But he pulled the mask back on and gave me a smile. "This isn't just about you and Miranda not killing each other. It's also important that you be okay. That you deal with the bad things that have happened, and…"

"Yeah," I interrupted. "I'll go to the counselor, and if he or she isn't totally annoying, I'll make an effort. Okay?"

He sighed as if he realized that he'd gotten all he was going to get out of me. "Yeah. Okay. And, look, Karen, if you need somebody to talk to, before we get all that set up…"

"I'm fine." I pinned a big smile on my face. *See?* I wanted to tell him. *I'm trying to fit in. I'm learning to be just as fake as the rest of you*. But that didn't seem like something that would end a conversation, and I was ready for this to be over.

"We also need to talk about you going out alone. Especially at night. It's not safe. I understand that you get upset, but we need to know where you are."

It was a little damn late for him to start acting like a

caring parent. I shook my head. "It's not like this is a rough town. And I have a phone; if I run into trouble, I'll call the cops."

"The trouble you run into might not *let* you use your phone."

"We learned about this in sociology class; you're falling for the 'stranger danger' myth. People *think* that it's danger- ous to be out alone, but the vast majority of violent inci- dents take place inside the home. I'm safer out there than I am in here, statistically." I held up my arms so he could see the bandages. "And the theory's supported by recent experi- ences, too."

"Sore elbows are not the big risk here."

"I'm fine," I insisted. "And there's no way I'm sitting around this house forever, and since I don't know anybody up here, I don't have much *choice* about going out alone."

"Well, that's something we should probably try to change," he said with a confident nod of his head. "Matt and Miranda have plenty of friends, and maybe it's time they in- troduced you to them. In fact, they're going to some sort of party tonight, a 'last weekend of freedom' thing before school starts. I think you should go with them and get to know people."

"That's a terrible idea," I said firmly. "Did you not just hear what Natalie said about me and Miranda staying away from each other?"

"You wouldn't have to hang out with her," he protested. "Matt could introduce you around."

Matt hadn't been openly hostile yet, but he and his sister were close. I had no doubt that he had the same problems with me that she did. Whatever they were. "I don't think so," I said. "But thanks for thinking of me. I'm just going to watch some TV."

"Karen…"

"My arms are really sore," I said, holding up my bent and bandaged limbs as proof. "*And* I took painkillers earlier. There's almost certainly going to be some sort of alcohol at this party, right? So I'd have to either be the loser who won't even sip a beer, or I'd risk a drug interaction. Alcohol and painkillers…that can't be good, can it?" I gave him about a second to find a rebuttal, then headed for the basement.

I was flipping channels, trying to find anything worth watching on TV, when Will appeared on the stairs.

He was halfway down before I noticed that there was another pair of legs coming down behind him, and when I saw the expression on his face, I knew something was up. "You have a visitor," he said cautiously, and then the person behind him came into view.

I sat up straighter and wondered desperately whether I had food stains from dinner on the front of my dress. "Tyler. Hi."

"Hey," he said. He sounded casual, but friendly, I was pretty sure. I mean, he was there…that meant that he was a friend, didn't it? Was it just friends? Was he *too* casual? Were we just running-and-swimming friends, and he thought maybe he'd add a little TV watching to our schedule? If he actually *liked* me, he'd probably be more nervous, right? Unless he was just a confident person…

"Do you want to sit down?" My voice sounded more or less normal.

He glanced at Will as if for permission, then crossed the room on his long, strong legs. He was wearing loose jeans and another one of his faded T-shirts, the thin cotton draping just right across his shoulders and falling off his pecs. His brown hair was a little long and kind of flopped in his eyes, and he was absolutely gorgeous. I wanted to jump him, and maybe he could tell, because he sort of perched on the side of the couch instead of sinking back into the cushions.

"Sorry I didn't call—I think the number's unlisted, maybe, and I didn't know your cell."

"No problem," I managed.

"I just, uh…there's a party tonight, pretty big, at the beach. I thought you might want to go. Or maybe you've already got plans… Obviously this is late notice." He looked at me, and there was something in his eyes that made me realize he *was* a bit nervous; he was just really, really good at seeming calm.

That gave me more courage. "This is my big plan," I said with a cautious attempt at waving my arms around the room. "Watching TV. And there isn't even anything good on."

"Of course not," he said with a shrug. "It's Friday night, in the summer time. The TV people know that everyone's going to be at parties at the beach."

"Too bad about those arms, Karen," Will said with an evil grin. He turned to Tyler. "I was trying to persuade her to give the party a try, earlier, but she had some really good points. Turns out it wouldn't be safe for her to go out tonight."

Tyler looked at me closely, trying to judge how serious this all was. I had long sleeves on, but he squinted at them as if he had x-ray vision. "What's wrong with your arms? You okay?"

"I'm *fine*," I said with a withering look in Will's direction. "Just some scratches. A party might be a good way to get my mind off of things."

"But what about the possibility of alcohol?" Will asked in an overly concerned tone. "The drug interaction?"

Tyler clearly knew this was part of something else, and he just leaned back and let us go. I shook my head at Will. "It's been a while since I took a pill. I'm sure I'm fine."

Finally, Will nodded, then looked back to Tyler. "You driving? Not a drop of alcohol, if you're driving."

"I thought we could walk," Tyler said quickly. "It's not that far." He held his hands up defensively in front of him. "And I won't drink much, anyway."

"You'd better not. You've got practice tomorrow."

"Yes, sir," Tyler said seriously, and now it was the two of them who were on the same page and me who wasn't sure what they were talking about. I didn't really enjoy it.

But at least Will stopped being a pain about my change of heart, and he kept Tyler company while I went to get changed. I thought about Miranda's criticism of my wardrobe and considered pulling on a pair of jeans, but then I remembered that she was a crazy bitch and I didn't care what she said. My mom had loved sharing clothes with me, and she'd been big on personal style and avoiding the mass-produced look. I'd never cared that much until she was gone, but now it seemed important. So I found a long-sleeved dress with a lace-up bodice and a blazer in case it got cold. It was a vintage look, straight out of the eighties; I doubted there would be much appreciation for it in Corrigan Falls, but I liked it.

My hair I just piled on top of my head; there was no time for styling, and it would probably just get frizzy and wild near the water anyway. And it's not like I'd be able to do much of a comb-out with my twisted arms. I managed to stretch the scab on one of them enough to put on some funky beaded earrings and a bit of lip gloss and mascara. With that, I was as presentable as I ever got.

I went back to the rec room and Tyler and Will both stood up like I was a lady or something. It was fun, but I knew I couldn't carry it off for long. "Sorry for the wait," I said to Tyler. "You ready?"

"Absolutely." Then he shook Will's hand, a move that was even more vintage than my dress, and we all trooped up the stairs and toward the front door.

Of course, it couldn't be that easy, because just then Natalie and Miranda were emerging from the study. They both had red eyes and looked a bit beat up, so I guess their heart-to-heart had been more in-depth than Will's and mine.

Miranda took one look at Tyler, turned back to her mother with her mouth gaping like a goldfish, and then brushed past us and ran for the stairs.

Natalie glared at Will, who seemed just as confused by the whole thing as I was. "Damn it…" she started, but then she broke off and followed Miranda up the stairs.

I looked at Will, who shrugged in confusion. "Who knows?" He seemed happy to not be involved. "Karen, you've got your phone and some money? You'll call us if you need anything."

"I'm good," I agreed. "All set."

He frowned at Tyler. "Matt and Miranda are planning to go down to this thing, too." He glanced doubtfully over his shoulder. "Well, Matt at least. I'll tell him to look for you there and say hi."

"Does 'say hi' mean 'check in'?" I asked. Just when

Will was starting to be a little bit cool, he had to pull this. "Because I don't need a babysitter, and if I did, I don't think *Matt* would be the guy for the job."

"I'll keep an eye out for him, let him know where we are," Tyler said from behind me. I didn't like being talked over top of, and I would have elbowed him in the ribs if I wasn't pretty sure it would hurt me more than him. But I had to admit, Tyler saying that seemed to settle Will down, and we made it out of the house without further incident.

We walked quietly for about a block, and then Tyler said, "I asked around about you. After I dropped you off yesterday. I was curious, so I asked some people." He looked over at me. "So I know some stuff. I just…you know. I didn't want to have to pretend like I was all surprised if you told me something that I'd already heard."

I guess I appreciated his honesty, but that was about it. "You probably heard a lot of bullshit," I said. "Miranda's been telling her friends that I'm a stuck-up bitch."

"That's not what I heard," he said softly. "It was more… about your mom. About why you had to come live up here. I'm sorry."

"Oh, okay," I said quickly. "Don't worry about it." I refused to start crying, which meant I really shouldn't think about certain subjects. "I didn't ask anyone about you, so you can give it to me directly. Like, how do you know Will?"

"Mr. Beacon—Your dad." Tyler frowned like he was trying to wrap his brain around the multiple identities. "He's one of the team sponsors. He's pretty involved."

"You left out some steps, there. What team? What practice are you going to tomorrow?"

He walked quietly for longer than made sense for such a

simple series of questions, then stopped moving and turned to look me in the eye. "Straight up," he said, "you don't know what team I'm on? You haven't heard about any of this?"

"Jesus, Tyler, is it the X-Men? Because if it's anything short of superheroes, you're being kinda dramatic." But he didn't laugh, just kept looking at me, and finally I shook my head and returned his gaze. "I have no idea what team you're on. I hadn't said a word to you or about you before yesterday, and right after you dropped me off last night Miranda and I got into a huge fight. We haven't had time for gossiping about boys."

He watched my face for a moment longer, then grinned self-consciously. "You're right, I was being kinda dramatic. It's not a big deal. But I play for the Raiders." He waited for a reaction, but all he got was a blank stare. "Some people think that's impressive," he said.

"I don't even know what sport that is. *The Raiders*?"

It took him a moment, but then he laughed. I got the feeling it was more at himself than at me. "It's hockey," he said with a grin. "The OHL." He saw my expression and prompted, "The Ontario Hockey League? It's Major Junior hockey, one step below the NHL." Apparently I still wasn't giving him the right look because he added, "It's kind of a big deal! I'm the top scorer, team captain…"

"I don't really follow hockey," I said hesitantly.

He looked at me as if I'd said I didn't breathe air. "What do you mean?"

It was my turn to laugh. "What do *you* mean? You think everyone in the world loves hockey?"

"Everyone in *Canada*, at least!"

"I don't have anything against it. I just don't follow it."

It wasn't like I hadn't known hockey fans in the city, but I hadn't actually hung out with many of them. My mom's artistic dancer crowd wasn't all that into pro sports, and I guess most of my friends were kind of the same way.

We started walking again and Tyler took some time to digest what I'd told him. But apparently he was still having trouble. "Like, if I asked you who won the Stanley Cup last year…"

"I know what the Stanley Cup *is*. I know people get excited about it way too late in the year, when it's already practically summer time and I can't understand why anyone's still playing hockey. But, no, I have no idea who won. I don't know who played. I could probably name a few teams in the league if I had to, but…that's about it." I was starting to get nervous. I really liked this guy. And everybody knows girls are supposed to care about the same things their boyfriends care about. Not that Tyler was my boyfriend, but…a girl could dream. Was I screwing all this up by not liking hockey? "I maybe just don't know enough about it," I tried. "I'm sure it's a good game."

"It's a great game," he said with the quiet confidence of someone stating common knowledge. "But…" he looked over at me with a crooked grin. "It's not your thing. That's fine." He nodded as if confirming to himself that it was okay. "It's kind of cool, actually. I mean, it's nice to be with someone with some perspective on it all. Does that make sense?"

"I guess?" It seemed like I was going to get away with this, but I didn't want to screw it up by saying the wrong thing now. "But one step below the NHL? And you're the top scorer? That's good, right?"

"Well, I used to think so," he said with exaggerated

sensitivity. "Now, it doesn't seem too great, all of a sudden."

"Poor princess," I said, and I gave him a hip check that ended up brushing my elbow against his. I sucked a pained breath of air in through my teeth, and of course he noticed.

"Your arm?" he asked concernedly. "What happened?"

It was strange, but I didn't want to tell him. Not because I was ashamed, or because I wanted it to be a secret, but just because it seemed like time for it to be over. I had no idea what was going on with Miranda, but I was pretty sure Sara was right; there was more to this than just having trouble adjusting to a new person in the family. She'd obviously been miserable, back at the house, and I wasn't cruel enough to take that as a personal victory. It was time for me to move on. So I just shrugged. "Wiped out on concrete and scratched up my elbows. Not one of my more graceful moments."

"You scratched your elbows...you wiped out *backwards*?" He was clearly trying to picture it in his mind and having some difficulty. "How'd you manage that?"

"I'm like a ninja," I said seriously. "I have special skills."

"Skills that let you fall over backwards on concrete."

"They don't come in handy all that often," I admitted, "but when I need them, I'll be ready."

"Okay," he said calmly. "That's good to know." We walked on in friendly silence for a while, and it wasn't long before we could see the flames of several bonfires and hear music and laughing and fun.

But now that we were so close, I was suddenly shy. I wasn't a huge partier at the best of times, and this was far from the best. I was with a hot guy, and he seemed nice, but I barely knew him, and I didn't know *anyone* else. Which would have been fine, if none of them had known me. But I thought of the girls in the drugstore the day before and wondered how many other people had heard Miranda's version of my life. "Who did you ask?" Tyler looked at me blankly, so I clarified. "When you were curious about why I was living at the Beacons'. Who did you ask?"

"A friend's girlfriend. Why?"

"It's just weird, people I've never met thinking they know stuff about me."

Tyler's smile was sweet, but there was a little bit of teasing when he said, "Welcome to Corrigan Falls, Karen. Small towns are different." He nudged me gently with his hip, pushing me in the direction of the party. "Come meet people. They can get to know you themselves, and then they won't have to bother with gossiping."

"Yeah." It sounded good, in principle, and I let him guide me forward. It was an opportunity, I told myself. This was my new life.

I just had to get used to it.

Chapter Twelve

I led Karen along a grassy path between the dunes and we came out onto the beach. There was a big bonfire in the middle of the space, and a few smaller fires around the edges, but there was no other light. The breeze was cool coming in off the lake, but I knew it'd be warm near the fires. Karen stopped walking and looked around, and I remembered my own reaction to my first Corrigan Falls beach party. The town was plain and a bit ragged during the day, but on nights like this? The whole scene felt like something from a movie.

"It looks more like a bunch of little parties," Karen said. Maybe she'd been a little less impressed by it all than I had been. After all, she was from the city, and probably went to big events all the time.

"It's still early," I said. I didn't want to sound defensive, but it was true. "People are in their groups, getting warmed up. Once it gets busier, and everyone gets drunker, they'll mix more." I hadn't realized how much I valued all this until just then, as I worried that she wouldn't like it.

"I don't have a group," she said quietly. "Can I borrow yours?"

"Absolutely." I guided her across the sand toward the team, but she was still looking around like she wasn't totally comfortable.

"People are staring at us," she whispered.

I'd gotten so immune that I hadn't noticed. "I told you," I said lightly, "I'm a big deal. Very important. People care what I do." She didn't look convinced, which I still really liked. "Plus, you're new. Everyone's curious. Don't worry about it."

I let my fingers brush against hers, just to see her reaction, and then did it again. She looked up at me, one eyebrow raised, and I grinned back at her as I took her hand more firmly. "Okay?" I asked.

"Okay," she agreed, and squeezed my fingers tighter than I'd expected.

"Mac Daddy!" a familiar voice called out, and I turned my head, then raised my free hand in acknowledgement.

"Winslow!" I called back, and steered Karen in that direction. "He's a good guy," I said quietly as we got closer. "Some of the team...they're a bit rough. But Winslow's okay."

"Hey, dude," Winslow said, reaching out a hand and giving me a fist-bump. "You made it. Good. It's a team thing."

"It's a kegger, and three quarters of the team is underage," I corrected. "You make sure the coaches don't hear you saying it's for the team."

"Yeah, yeah," Winslow said dismissively. Then he turned to Karen. "Chris Winslow," he said, and nodded to the dark-haired girl nestled under his arm. "And this is Terri."

"Tori," she corrected. She shrugged at Karen as if they should both understand he couldn't be expected to know better, and I cringed. Winslow was bad at names. He'd only learned mine after I'd pointed out the fast food connection, and he still wasn't sure about most of the rookies on the team. But Karen didn't know that, and she might think he'd gotten Tori's name wrong because he was an uncaring asshole who treated women like they were interchangeable. And I didn't want her to think that about him. Or about me.

"I'm Karen," she said, cutting through all my stupid angsting with an easy smile.

"Karen's a friend of mine," I told Winslow, putting just a little extra emphasis on the word 'friend'. He'd know what that meant.

Winslow gave her another look and then nodded slowly. "Nice to meet you." He half turned and gestured into the shadows. "The keg's in the truck bed. Help yourselves." He looked at Karen, then me. "Dawn's got a bunch of coolers and stuff, too, if you want. I think they're in the cab of the truck."

"Thanks," I said. He'd gotten my message clear enough. I didn't let go of Karen's hand as I guided her toward the truck. "You want a cooler?"

"Beer's fine," she said, then added, "I'm not a huge drinker."

"I don't know if that is going to work for you up here. Once it gets cold, drinking's about all there is to do at night."

"No TV, this far north? No books? No conversation, or

video games, or cooking classes?"

I squinted at her. "Cooking classes? That's what you think's going to keep you busy?"

"Yeah, that was a weird thing to say," she admitted with a grin. "I just thought of it because my best friend in the city loves to cook. She was always trying to get me to take classes with her. But usually I'd just go to her house and eat her homework."

"I don't understand that. Isn't cooking, like…don't you just follow the recipe? Why do you need a class?" I pulled a couple plastic cups from a stack in the bed of the truck and held one under the tap of the keg.

"There're techniques," Karen said. "Like, you're pouring a beer, right? The recipe might just say 'pour a beer', but you have a way of doing it. Tilting the cup, letting the beer hit the side first…whatever. That's the kind of stuff she'd learn. *And* recipes."

"I like the 'eat the homework' idea." I handed her a filled cup and then poured my own before reclaiming her hand. It felt natural, like it just made sense for us to be touching each other. "Come on," I said. "I'll introduce you to some people."

And that was when things got kind of stressful. Because practically everyone in town was at the party, at least everyone between about fifteen and twenty-five, and there were quite a few people in that age category that I didn't really want Karen to talk to. Which was stupid, because it had been my idea to come to the party in the first place, and I'd known who would be there. I guess I just hadn't thought it through. Everything seemed so simple when it was just me and Karen, but I should have known things would get complicated once other people were added to the mix.

I'd have to face my past sooner or later, but for tonight, at least, I didn't want to. So I steered Karen through the party like we were playing that old video game where the frog has to get across the road. We'd hop a little bit forward, say 'hi' to a few people, and then I'd spot trouble coming and we'd jump a few spots to the left, finding another group for a quick greeting and then someone else would approach and I'd tug Karen away, trying to keep us from getting splatted by a big frog-killing truck.

Not quite what I'd had in mind when I'd suggested Karen come out with me. Maybe I should have suggested we do something with just the two of us, but it had seemed too early for that, somehow. Which made no sense, because we'd already spent a whole afternoon alone together, but that had been kind of accidental. This? Showing up at her house, talking to her dad, even. It felt like a date. And I was pretty sure it felt the same way to her, but I wasn't totally positive, and if she *did* feel that way I wanted her to keep thinking of it that way. A date, not a hook up. Something that might be the start of something. That's what I was hoping she was seeing tonight.

"You know a lot of people," she said after we'd made several hops. "But who are you really *friends* with?"

"The team," I said without hesitation. "Winslow, and Coop—I haven't seen him yet, but he'll be around somewhere. I'm pretty tight with most of them, I guess."

"But we haven't been hanging out with them tonight?"

No, because the team was at the center of all the speeding vehicles my frog was trying to avoid. But that wasn't something I wanted to explain to Karen, so I just shrugged.

"I spend a lot of time with them already. It's nice to have a change."

So, there it was. I lied to her. Not a big lie, but I was hiding something I shouldn't have been hiding, and it didn't feel good at all.

Chapter Thirteen

Tyler and I roamed all over the beach, until everything turned into a blur of unfamiliar faces, a cacophony of new names, and too many subtle interactions and reactions for me to begin to keep track of. He repeated the phrase "my friend" with the same special emphasis to practically every guy we met, and it began to get on my nerves. Was he making it clear that he wasn't really interested in me? I mean, I'd thought the hand-holding meant something, but maybe he was just touchy-feely? I wasn't as flashy as most of the other girls, that was for sure. I felt mousy, my dress too conservative compared to their outfits, my hair too simple, my make-up more appropriate for the gym than for a party. Maybe the hand-holding didn't mean as much as I was hoping it did; maybe he just wanted to keep track of me in the crowd.

He eventually released me when I had to go to the

bathroom. I walked to the concrete building with a couple other girls, and I listened to them talking as we stood in line. They'd apparently come to the party with each other, but were hoping to leave with guys, preferably hockey players.

"Too bad you already scooped Tyler up," one of them said to me. She didn't sound hostile, just resigned. "I almost had him last spring, and I was totally planning to close the deal tonight." She shrugged. "Oh well. Next time."

"He's worth the wait," the other girl said. "I would absolutely go back for second helpings of him." She turned to me. "You're going to have a *good* time." Their laughter was somewhere between giggles and cackling, and I was incredibly relieved when a stall door swung open and I was able to take the excuse to get away from them.

I bolted the thin metal door behind me and tried to figure it out. Mostly, I tried to think of a way for them to have been talking about something other than what I *thought* they were talking about, but I couldn't do it. One of those girls had come to this party with plans to have sex with Tyler, and the other one already *had*, and would be happy to do it again. No shyness, no broken hearts, just…sex.

With Tyler.

I went through the motions in the stall, my mind far away, and when I was done I bent over a sink and splashed water on my face, trying to cool down. Was this what Tyler was expecting from me? Casual sex, no attachment, no real feelings, just…what had the first girl said? *Closing the deal*.

I saw one of the girls come out of her stall and head for the sink, but I didn't wait for her. I'd only had two beers over a couple hours, but I suddenly felt dizzy, and my brain wasn't working properly. I wasn't a virgin. I'd had a serious boyfriend in the spring, and we'd ended up having sex a few times before having a stupid fight and breaking up. He'd been cute, but nothing like Tyler. If Tyler expected sex tonight, was I prepared to go through with it? I wasn't ready for it, psychologically, but maybe that didn't matter. If sex was what it took to keep him in my life, and if I *did* want him, then maybe it wasn't that big of a deal to just go a little faster than I'd be completely comfortable with.

It felt wrong, but it felt wrong to think about walking away from him, too. Or watching him walk away from me, when he realized that I was just a scared little kid, not a sophisticated woman like these others. I pushed through the crowd and found my way down to the lake. The air was cool, but I kicked my sandals off and waded in up to my ankles. I was tempted to just keep going, to swim away from the confusion, but I knew it would just follow after me. And of course, I started thinking about my mom, and how good she'd been about all this stuff. I'd talked to her about sex last time, and she'd been calm and accepting, letting me know she thought I should take it slow, but not making me feel like a slut. She'd been the best mom ever, and now she was gone. But I wasn't ready to be alone; I still needed her.

"You okay?"

I turned to the shore and saw Tyler, silhouetted against the light of the campfire. I thought of his gentle smile and quiet humor and tried to reconcile it with what the girls had said.

"I don't know," I answered.

He was wearing jeans, but he didn't even hesitate before wading out to me, the water soaking the cuffs of his pants. At least he'd just had sport sandals on, so he wasn't ruining his shoes. Still, I felt like an idiot, someone who constantly needed rescuing and caretaking.

"No, I'm fine," I said, and when he got close I took a step back, away from him.

He stopped moving. "What happened?"

"I'm just being stupid. Sorry." But I still didn't want to touch him, and he seemed to be able to tell.

"Do you want to go home? I can walk you home if you want."

"So you can come back and hook up with somebody else?" I snarled. Apparently I'd decided to address this head on. If Tyler was just a junior version of Will, I needed to know now. "That girl with the white shorts, maybe. She said she'd be interested. Or her friend. I guess you've already slept with her, but she seemed like she'd be happy with another round."

Tyler's jaw literally dropped. He looked adorably con-fused, the moonlight casting dark shadows beneath his cheekbones, his eyes wide with surprise. "Shit," he finally said. "I didn't think they'd move in so fast."

"What? Move in?" I shook my head. "Is that true, Tyler? I mean, Miranda kept implying that you're…you know. A bit promiscuous. But I thought she was just being bitchy. I don't…this is freaking me out, Tyler."

He nodded slowly. "Yeah. I can see that. I'm sorry."

"But it's true. You…" I wasn't sure how to put it into words. "That's what you do. You sleep with lots of girls, just one-night-stands, just…"

"Karen," he said as if he wanted my attention, but once I gave it to him he didn't seem to have much to say. Finally, he said, "Yeah. I guess. I mean, it's the hockey. That's why they're interested. They're puck bunnies, you know?"

I stared at him for a moment, trying to wrap my ears around what he seemed to have said. I couldn't do it. "They're *what*?"

He looked uncomfortable. "Puck bunnies. Like…like hockey groupies."

"You have groupies. And they're called 'puck bunnies.'" It was sinking in, but it wasn't making much sense.

"That's the more polite term. You don't want to hear the others." He looked like he knew this wasn't going over too well with me, but he kept talking. "This is my third year in the league. The first two years…it kind of went to my head, I guess. I was sixteen, living away from home and hanging out with guys who did the same things, and these girls—women, sometimes—they were throwing themselves at me, and…I caught a lot of them. It was fun, and everybody knew the rules."

"The rules?"

"That it's not something serious. It's not a *relationship*, or anything, it's just fun."

"Sex," I clarified.

He shrugged uncomfortably. "Yeah. Usually. But always with protection. I was always really careful about that."

"How many…" I started, but I caught myself. "No. I don't want to know." At least the conversation had clarified one thing for me. "I'm not like that. I mean, these girls… I'm not going to call them what you call them, I don't think. I mean, is it an insult? It sounds like an insult."

"Puck bunny? I don't know. Like I said, it's the most polite word I know for them."

"But they're not, like, a club. They're individual people.

Calling them all by the same name, it seems… I don't like it."

He frowned thoughtfully. "Okay. Most of the girls I've gone out with have a habit of sleeping with hockey players. Is that better?"

"And you have a habit of sleeping with lots of girls," I said pointedly.

He nodded slowly, accepting responsibility. "Yeah. I guess so."

"I'm not like that." I honestly hadn't been sure until I heard myself say the words, but once they were out of my mouth I knew they were true. I liked Tyler, a lot, but I'd seen too much of Will to let myself turn into Natalie. "If that's at all what you're expecting, then, yeah, I guess you should walk me home now, because it's not going to happen."

But he shook his head. "No. That's not what I'm expecting. You're not a…" He stopped and frowned at me, searching for more acceptable words. "That's not what I expect from you."

"But it's what people expect from you," I said slowly, thinking of Miranda's accusations. "And if I'm with you…"

"The guys know. When I told them you were my friend, they knew. It's like a code, kind of. That's why Winslow offered you a cooler—the keg's good enough for—" he caught himself again, shook his head in frustration, and said, "good enough for some people. But girlfriends get coolers."

I wasn't sure whether to laugh or cry. Hearing the word *girlfriend* come out of his mouth, referring to me, should have made me ecstatic. But the ridiculous ranking of human beings, the matter-of-fact way he was talking about all the casual sex he'd had…it was overwhelming. "Okay," I said. "I'm still freaking out a bit. I mean, I like you. I've had fun with you. But I don't know if I'm ready for something like this. You know?"

"I should have kept you to myself," he said quietly. "We could have gone swimming, and driven up the peninsula, and kept running together. I should have kept you away from all this crap."

"It was just a matter of time," I said slowly. "School starts soon, and lord knows Miranda's been looking for any excuse to trash you. I would have found out sooner or later."

"But later would have been better. I would have had more time to prove to you that I'm past that."

"Are you? Why? I mean, if it was so much fun, why do you want to quit?"

He frowned at me. "I want something different, I guess. I don't need to have fun all the time, not if it's getting in the way of something bigger. Screwing around with…whatever you want to call them…it was fine while it lasted, but now I want something more."

He was saying all the right things. But I wasn't sure if it was enough. "My head's spinning," I confessed. "I think I should go home. Thanks for thinking of me tonight." Saying the words was hard, but once they were out, I felt better. Going home was an excellent idea, and I started determinedly toward the shore.

Tyler followed after me. "I'll walk you," he said.

"No, you don't have to."

"We don't have to talk. Or, if you don't want to be seen with me, I can walk half a block behind, or something. But I should walk you, or you should call your dad for a ride. It's Friday night, and there's lots of drunk assholes out looking for trouble."

"And what about the other girls? Who's going to make sure *they* get home safely?"

He snorted in exasperation. "They can get home the same way they got out, just like you can. I can't be responsible for everyone, Karen, but I should be responsible for you. I asked you to come, so I should see you home."

He really did seem like a decent guy. And a total slut who used girls like they were toys. I had no idea what to do with the contradiction.

So we walked home in silence, and I tried not to miss the feel of his fingers wrapped around mine. When we got to the sidewalk in front of the house, we stopped walking and he said, "I missed running today because we had fitness testing at practice; I needed to save my energy. But I'll be there tomorrow. Will you be there?"

"I have no idea," I said, and I turned and walked slowly toward the house.

Chapter Fourteen

"You're back early," Natalie said when I slipped through the back door into the kitchen. "Matt just left, and you're already home? Was it not fun?" The words were light, but she was watching me closely, as if she expected something much worse than just *not fun*.

Miranda was sitting with her at the table, and they both had bowls with the remnants of what looked like ice cream sundaes in front of them. Apparently when these girls had a heart-to-heart, they didn't mess around. Miranda kept her eyes on her spoon.

"It was okay," I said noncommittally. "But I didn't know anyone, and it got to be a bit much."

"You want to sit down with us? Have some ice cream?"

Miranda's glare at her mother was hard to miss.

"No, thanks. I'll just go to bed, I think."

"Karen…" Natalie started. She looked at Miranda, then back at me. "I think we need to talk about Tyler."

"Because Miranda doesn't like him? He's been nothing but sweet to me." It was strange how fast my own hesitations were overwhelmed by my urge to prove Miranda wrong.

Natalie nodded slowly. "That's important. And good to know. But you're new to town, and I just want to make sure you have all the facts before you make any decisions that could affect your time here."

"What does that mean?" I asked.

Miranda stood abruptly. "I don't need to be here for this," she said. It looked like her eyes were filling again.

"Okay," Natalie said slowly. "But it might be good if you and Karen talked about it at some point."

"Like she'd listen," Miranda sneered. "She thinks—"

"Stop," Natalie said firmly. "We're not doing that anymore. No more talking about other people, no more saying what someone else thinks when you don't know for sure."

Miranda glared at her mother, then shrugged. "Fine. I'm going to bed, then. Have fun with your talk. I'm sure it'll go *really* well."

She stomped out of the room, and Natalie looked up at me with a tight, tired smile. "Sit?"

I sat. "I'm not even your kid," I said. "You're stuck sorting through all this crap, and Will isn't even helping. Doesn't that piss you off?"

The smile shifted from tight to absolutely rigid. "Let's focus on you, for now."

"So, you can poke into my business, but I'd better stay the hell out of yours?" It wasn't like I was actually interested in the intricacies of her marriage, but the double standard seemed like something we could acknowledge.

And she did just that. "Exactly," she said. "So, Tyler. I don't really know him. I know he's a star player and everyone thinks he's heading for the big leagues, and I've met him at a few team functions, but that's about it."

"He's nice," I said defensively.

"And cute," she added.

I decided it might be time for a little pushing. "Cute is for puppies. Tyler MacDonald is hot."

"And from what I'm hearing, he takes advantage of that fact." She didn't sound judgmental, exactly, but it didn't feel like she was celebrating his resourcefulness, either.

"From what I saw tonight, being good looking is just the icing. The cake is being a hockey player. This town is kind of insane about that team." That was true. There had been quite a few guys around the team keg who were no kind of handsome, and they'd still been getting plenty of attention.

"Either way," Natalie said carefully, "Tyler's had a lot of experience with girls. He's been seen with a lot of girls." She seemed to be searching for the right words.

I decided to help her out. "He's had sex with a lot of girls."

"Sounds like it." She looked down at her bowl as if she wished there was still ice cream in it.

"So?" I made it sound like a challenge, but really I think I was asking for her opinion. What *was* I supposed to feel, now that I knew this about Tyler?

She looked up at me, her expression sincere. "So is that the kind of boy you want to be with? To be *seen* with? You're new to town, and the situation is unusual enough that people are curious. If they see you with someone like that, they're going to make assumptions about you that may not be accurate. But the opinions can last a long time, even after…"

"Even after Tyler dumps me?"

"Or you dump him, or whatever happens. It sounds like he's not much good at long-term relationships. And maybe that's fine. He's a teenage boy, and he's probably dazzled by the bright future everyone is promising; I'm not expecting him to be settling down and getting serious. But it'd be a shame for you to ruin your reputation over someone you might not even be talking to next week."

"*Ruin my reputation*?" She'd been trying to be tactful, but she'd taken it too far. "What is this, the fifties?"

"It's a small town, Karen. You don't have the same kind of anonymity that you had in Toronto. Your reputation is a real thing up here, and it's fragile."

"Wow. It's nice to know your family cares about that. Except Miranda's already told the whole town I'm a bitch, so I guess my reputation's already in trouble; they might as well think I'm a slut, too." And since Natalie wasn't quick to respond, I added, "Is all of this crap that you're hearing about Tyler coming from Miranda? What is her problem with him, anyway?"

Natalie didn't answer, but there was something about the *way* she didn't answer that suddenly made things clear.

"She slept with him," I said. It felt like the words were coming from outside of me. "She's been going around calling *him* a slut — "

"We don't use that word!" Natalie almost yelled. She looked toward the front hall, where the stairs led to the upper floor. Luckily, there was no sign of Miranda. "Nobody's a 'slut'. It's an ugly word, and there's no need to judge other people based on personal decisions they've made."

"Unless it's Tyler. It's okay to judge him." It was easier to be angry than confused.

"If someone's made the same decision, time and time again, it would be naïve to expect them to make a different decision at the next opportunity. That's all."

"Maybe it's the same decision *I've* made. Maybe it'd be fine for the town to think I'm easy, because maybe I am."

"I'm not sure 'easy' is any better than 'slut,' really," she mused. I guess it was simpler to worry about the words instead of the idea of what I'd said. She seemed to realize she was wimping out and shrugged her way back to the topic at hand. "You're here. School starts in a few days, and you'll meet all kinds of new people. I'm not going to try to tell you what to do, but I hope you'll think about it. I'm sorry Miranda has said things about you that you don't like, and—"

"Wait a second. *That I don't like,* as if I'm being over-sensitive or something? She totally slammed me. And that wasn't enough, so now she's got you picking on Tyler. It's bullshit to call me naïve for thinking he might make differ-ent decisions; sometimes, people change, and it's not *naïve* to give them a chance." I stood up. "I don't give a shit what your precious town thinks about me. The only person in this whole place who's been nice to me is Tyler. He's given *me* a chance, and I am absolutely going to do the same with him."

Natalie nodded slowly. "We've made a mess of this," she said, almost to herself. She looked up at me as if I had something she needed. "We had the best of intentions." She frowned. "*I* had the best of intentions." Another frown, be-fore the last one had even faded away. "For Will. For me, and the family." She looked up at me again. "I thought he needed to take responsibility for you. Before the accident, he'd always sent child support, but that was just…it wasn't even a check, just an automatic withdrawal from the bank account. I used to think of it as an irresponsibility tax. I wanted him to get to know you, as a person, and to be a better father. To realize that he'd created a life and should be involved with it. But I didn't give enough thought to how all this would affect *you*."

It should have been a moment of victory for me, but it didn't really feel that way. I sat back down. "It's not your fault," I said. "It's not like I had anywhere else to go."

"Not boarding school? Or staying with friends? I recall you suggesting both of those options."

"Staying with friends?" I have no idea why, but apparently I'd decided to be honest. "I only had one close friend, and she's in Israel for the year, living with her dad. Her mom's taking most of the year to travel. So, no, I couldn't actually stay with friends." Natalie's face was carefully neutral, and I couldn't tell what she was hoping to hear me say. "It might not be too late for boarding school, though, if you want to get rid of me."

She shook her head. "I don't. At all. But I'm sorry things aren't going more smoothly for you here."

Damn, the woman was going to have me serving up ice cream and caramel sauce to go with our salty tears, if I wasn't careful. So I smiled brightly. "No worse than anywhere else. Boarding schools have a lot of rules, I think. And no hot hockey players."

She returned my smile, although hers was more subdued. "I asked Miranda if Tyler had forced her, or pressured her." Her hand was shaking a little as we both stared at the spoon she was toying with. "She said no. She said she'd never heard that about him. Apparently…" She took a deep breath. "Apparently my precious daughter was all too willing to give up her virginity to a one-night-stand." She set the spoon down and looked at me. "Although, of course, 'giving up virginity' is also an outmoded expression, and I should celebrate my family as they blossom into their adult sexuality…" Now it was her turn to stand abruptly, and she scooped the bowls off the table and carried them purposefully to the sink. "Sorry. That was more than you needed to hear."

"Did he lie to her?" I wanted to know for Miranda's sake, but also for my own. "Did he make her believe it was something more? Like, did she think they were dating?"

The bowls hit the stainless steel sink with a clatter. "No," she said without turning to look at me. "Not from what she said tonight." We were silent for a while, and then she came back over and sat down. "But I think she wanted it to be more," she said softly. "I think she thought…you know. That it was a logical step toward their happy ending. I think that's why she reacted so poorly to your relationship with him."

"We've never even kissed," I said quickly. I wasn't sure why it was important, but I wanted her to know. "He hasn't… He held my hand tonight, and it was like he was *nervous* about just that."

She nodded thoughtfully. "Okay. Look, Karen, I know I'm not your mom, but I feel like I kind of screwed this up with Miranda, and I really don't want to do that with you. Keep me informed, okay? I don't mean details, just… I don't want to find out about these things six months after they happened, if I can avoid it. And I'm reasonably good to talk to, I think. I hope."

"You're good," I agreed. "But, look… I'm not a virgin. We don't have to worry about that big conversation, or anything."

"And did you talk to your mother about that decision, when you made it?"

"Yeah. I did."

"I've been angry at her for a long time, you know." God, once this woman got started with the soul-searching, she kept going. But it wasn't like she didn't have a right to be pissed. "I shouldn't have been," she said, contradicting my internal reaction. "I should have been angry at Will. And I was. But I had to forgive him in order to make our lives work, and I didn't have to forgive her. So I didn't."

"I know she felt bad about you. And the twins. She didn't know about any of you, at the time. He told her he'd left his wife, but he didn't say you were pregnant."

"I know," she said. "I hadn't told him before he left, but even after I did tell him, he still—" She stopped, as if realizing who she was talking to, and shook her head to get back on topic. "It sounds like maybe Tyler is trying to grow up a little. But some boys never really do."

It wasn't my place to comment on that, and I wouldn't have had any idea what to say if she'd asked me to. So I stood up. "I'm going to bed. I'll try to… I have no idea where things are going with Tyler. Maybe nowhere. If something *does* happen, I can try not to rub Miranda's nose in it, but I don't want to be sneaking around."

"You should do what's best for you, with Tyler. I expect he's pretty busy with the team, but if this seems like it's going somewhere, I'd like to get to know him better. And Miranda—she'll have to…" Natalie shook her head. "I'm her mom. I want to shield her from all this. But I guess she'll have to learn to deal with the consequences of her decisions." She didn't sound too satisfied with that resolution, but she didn't say anything to indicate that she was going to reconsider it.

I didn't think I needed to stick around and ask too many questions. Persuading Natalie to give Tyler a chance had helped soothe my own doubts, and I wanted to see him again. Immediately. Natalie busied herself tidying up the ice cream, and I sat there at the kitchen table, wondering what came next.

I thought about finding my way back down to the party, but it didn't seem like a good idea. I remembered what he'd said about drunk assholes being out in force, but I also thought about the girls in the bathroom, talking about hooking up with him like it was no big deal. He didn't owe me anything. If he'd walked me home and then gone back to the beach to find one of them, there was nothing I could say about it. But I didn't want to see it, or think about it.

That was when it hit me. Tyler was notorious for sleeping around. Just like my dad. And I was planning to overlook it, ignore it, just like Natalie did.

I wasn't sure what that meant. I wasn't exactly a Natalie fan, but I had to admit that she'd been making an effort to be good to me, in spite of all the things I'd said to hurt her. So maybe she was just a forgiving person, and I shouldn't be too judgmental since I was one of the people benefiting from her cheek-turning ways. But then I thought of how tight her face had been when I'd repeated what I'd heard in the drugstore. I thought about the whole town knowing that my father was cheating on her. They laughed about it; did they laugh *at* her? Some of them probably did.

But it wasn't like Tyler and I were married, or even going

out. I hadn't even been willing to commit to showing up for a run.

I had no claim on him. It was none of my business what, or who, he did. I nodded at Natalie and said, "Okay. Goodnight," and I went downstairs. It was hard not to imagine Tyler, his hair falling in his eyes as he directed his sexy grin at some other girl, as he let her hands run over his broad shoulders and down his tight chest and abs...

Damn it. I was pretty sure I'd made a huge mistake, walking away from him. It had felt right at the time, but obviously my brain could not be trusted on these matters. I pulled my dress off over my head and tossed it into the hamper, then flopped down on my bed. I ran my hand down my body, imagining that it was Tyler touching me, but it was no good. I kept picturing him with the bathroom girls, and then, even worse, Miranda, her perfect blond hair just a little mussed...

No. That image was not one I wanted in my brain.

For the millionth time that day, I wanted to talk to my mother. I wanted her to sit back on the ratty old sofa in our living room and pull me back to lean on her, just like she'd always done when I was upset. She'd smooth my hair away from my face and kiss me on the temple, and I'd feel safe and loved. We'd talk about it, and she'd mostly just listen. She'd ask questions, maybe, like she was really trying to figure it out, working through it with me.

That was what I wanted, and it was what I could never have. Thinking of that made all the nonsense with Tyler seem unimportant. My mother was gone. I was alone. Tyler was a distraction, but he wasn't one that I could afford. I was still too messed up, and I didn't need the complications.

He was a temptation I should try to resist.

Chapter Fifteen

- *TYLER* -

I hadn't wanted to go back to the party after dropping Karen off, so I just walked around for a while. I kept thinking about Karen, and about my past. I wondered if I'd change it, if I could. Would I give up all those girls, all those women, for a chance with a girl like Karen?

Well, I wouldn't have to give *all* of them up, I supposed. It wasn't like Karen was expecting me to be a complete virgin. She just wasn't looking for a total manwhore, either.

And that made me mad, for about a block of walking. I mean, she didn't like people judging the puck bunnies for the choices *they* made, but she was going to judge *me* for the things *I'd* done. At least my activities were in the past, and I'd learned something from them. The puck bunnies were still going strong, and if I headed back down to the beach I could probably have one of them in my truck inside of five minutes. Hell, I could've probably had two or three of them. It didn't seem fair that I wasn't getting any credit at all for showing a little restraint and *not* taking advantage of what was being offered.

Yeah, that lasted for about a block. Then I remembered how confused and hurt Karen had looked, and the resentment faded out of me pretty damn fast. One of the things that I liked about her was the way she saw things from the outside and didn't buy into the whole hockey-heroes thing. So I couldn't turn around and *stop* liking that about her just because she didn't give me the hockey-player immunity I was used to.

I wished she hadn't looked so good tonight. With her hair up and that old-fashioned dress on, she'd looked... I don't know. Delicate, I guess, except I'd run with her and knew how strong and fit she was, so I wasn't sure the word worked. Classy, for sure. That was a good one. But it wasn't all of it, because *classy* shouldn't be enough to have made me want to touch her all the time, which I totally did. Just holding her hand had been as memorable as full-out sex with some of the other girls I'd been with.

When I reached the park I started along the path we both followed. It was dark in the woods, the leaves cutting out most of the moonlight, but I knew the path well and the lack of light kind of fit my mood.

But obviously I shouldn't have been playing my emo game because I tripped over a root and fell forward, and my foot got caught somewhere behind me. For a split second, I thought I might actually hurt myself. Not a scraped knee, but an actual injury, something that would keep me on the sidelines for this, my big year where I was supposed to get scouted and drafted and go to the big league. And for that split second before my foot twisted free and I caught myself, I wasn't scared.

I was relieved.

I stood there alone in the forest, trying to make any sense out of that reaction. I'd spent my whole life working on making my body into a hockey machine, and now my brain was trying to sabotage all my efforts. Was that what my dad was seeing, what he was trying to warn me about? Sure, my dad was power tripping, but wasn't I being just as bad, acting like a rebellious little kid instead of a serious athlete?

If my attitude had deteriorated to the point where I was actually *happy* about the prospect of getting injured, then my attitude needed a readjustment. I would have to worry a little less about showing my dad who was boss and a little more about keeping myself on track. If I flaked out, it all would have been a waste. The missed birthday parties and school trips; the homework done in the back seat of the car, if it got done at all; the mornings I'd be on the ice before the sun came up, my mom sipping coffee in the stands with all the other dedicated parents; the afternoons I'd spend do-ing drills or practicing my shot instead of playing with the other kids; the nights spent watching videos, my dad point-ing out the strengths and weaknesses of other players; the early bedtime so I could get up the next morning and start all over again.

I was in my fifth year of high school because when my coaches had suggested I take six classes a year instead of eight, my parents hadn't even blinked. Hockey had been my life since the first time I'd strapped on a pair of skates, all in the service of the ultimate dream. If I didn't make the

NHL, I'd have nothing to show for the last *fifteen* years. My total reward for all that effort would be my two hundred and twenty dollars a week as an OHL player and a long list of barely remembered women who'd slept with me on the off chance that I might be somebody worth bragging about someday.

It was terrifying. Maybe that was why my brain was crapping out on me. Maybe it was trying to set up some defenses in case the worst happened. Because the truth was, I was a long way from a sure thing for the NHL. I was a solid player, but I wasn't the best at anything. I could skate better than most, but I wasn't the fastest guy out there, maybe not even the fastest on our team. I had a good shot, but I wasn't the absolute best sniper. I hit hard, made good plays, hustled, took abuse… I did it all well. Some years, the league was looking for strong all-round players. Other years, they wanted specialists. And even in a year where they *were* looking for all-rounders, was I one of the absolute best?

I wanted a drink. No, that wasn't quite right. I wanted a *lot* of drinks, and then I wanted to have a lot of sex, and then probably some more drinks, and then…yeah, probably then some more sex. I wanted to stop thinking about it all. I wanted to be distracted from the uncertainties, the things my dad pretended to be able to control with his bullshit about hard work and playing smart. The truth was that sometimes it didn't matter how hard you worked or how smart you played; sometimes, you still wouldn't be good enough, and there wasn't a damn thing you could do about that.

I turned around and headed out of the forest, walking fast but more carefully than I had on the way in. I wasn't going to let myself get injured. I wasn't going to take the easy way out. But I was absolutely going to find some alcohol. And I was going to try to use it to turn off my brain. If the beer wasn't enough…well, the beer and the puck bunnies were all in the same place. It seemed like the best place for me to be, too.

But I caught myself by the time I reached the street. I had no idea where things were with Karen. It was totally possible that things were blown forever, but maybe they weren't. But going back to the party and hooking up with someone? If Karen found out, *that* would be the end. And I didn't want to have to lie to her, didn't want to sneak around or worry about getting busted. We didn't have any secrets anymore, and I wanted to keep it that way.

So instead of turning toward the beach, I walked in the opposite direction. There were cars in the arena parking lot, enough to let me know what I was going to find when I went inside, and sure enough, there they were. The bar league hadn't really started up yet, but some of the teams had booked ice time for practices already. A bunch of guys, from just out of high school to retirement age, skating around, stick handling and shooting, playing our game and having a hell of a good time.

I climbed up into the stands and sat down. The sounds were a strange mix of familiar and exotic. I was used to the slap of sticks on ice, the grunts of men working hard, the crash of padded bodies into boards. But there were more laughing here, less yelling, and no whistle blowing to send the players to their next drills. They were sorting it all out for themselves, doing their own things at their own speeds. I was jealous.

I barely noticed when someone else climbed up into

the stands, but I turned to look when he sat down beside me. "Hey, Coach," I said. I wasn't sure what he was going to think about me hanging around the rink after hours. I was supposed to love the game, but I was supposed to be hanging out with the team and bonding, too.

But he didn't seem too concerned. "Any good prospects out there?" he asked lightly.

I shrugged. "Number seventy-two's got some hustle," I said. Number seventy-two's jersey number probably matched his age.

Coach nodded, and we both just sat there for a bit, watching. When a guy skated up to the boards and looked at us, I didn't recognize him, but I guess he knew us. "Hey, Coach," he said. "Hey, Tyler. You guys want to come show us how it's done?" A couple other players skated over and laughed, but they were staring at us like they were expecting an answer.

"You already seem to know what you're doing," Coach said. He was pretty good at being diplomatic. But he surprised me when he said, "But maybe we could come down and skate with you a bit." He turned to me and raised an eyebrow. "Unless you're too tired?"

I probably wasn't allowed to skate with them. I hadn't read my contract too carefully, but my dad and my agent had made it clear that it would be incredibly stupid to get injured playing a game I wasn't getting paid for. But if my coach said it was okay…. "I'm not too tired," I said.

I still wasn't sure if this was for real, but Coach stood up and pulled his locker room keys out of his pocket. "We'll go get changed," he said. "You guys have the ice for a while?"

"Another forty-five minutes."

So Coach and me put our gear on and went out on the ice. At first the other players were kind of over-respectful, almost shy, but then Coach started trash talking me and I got brave enough to throw a few playful insults back, and everybody relaxed. It was weird to think that these grown men had been intimidated by a kid like me, but that was the hockey mystique.

When Coach and I hit the ice, the practice turned into a sort of loose scrimmage, and it felt good to just skate and play. I tried a few tricks I'd seen on TV, and they mostly didn't work, but it was fun just to goof around. I played defense for a while, just for a change, skated backward and blocked shots and pretended to get mad when the other team's players didn't respect my goalie. Then I went back to my usual position as center, and I tried to make plays, tried to anticipate a game played at a different speed than the one I was used to. I didn't do a great job, but after one of my passes led to a goal, the scorer skated up to me and said, "I'm going to tell everybody about this when you hit the big league. I'm going to point to you on the TV screen and tell them about the time I got an assist from Tyler MacDonald the NHL star."

"*Star*, even," I said. I didn't want to be rude, but I really didn't need one more person making assumptions about my future that I wasn't sure I could live up to. "Not just making the league, but actually being a star. Damn. You're a bit of an optimist, huh?"

"Nope," he said with a confident grin. He glided away from me backward. "I've just got an eye for talent."

I tried not to let it bug me. I just wanted to *play*. I wanted to remind myself that even if the NHL didn't work out, I could still have this, could still skate around and take shots and have fun with my friends. But after the first guy said it, it seemed to set everyone else off, and they were all talking about the team's prospects for the season, what teams I wanted to play for in the NHL, whether I'd get called up after this year or be back in the development leagues next fall. It was all stuff that I had no control over, and I guess it was fun for *them* to wonder about it because it wasn't their lives they were talking about. For me? I wasn't sorry when the next team came out on the ice for their practice time and Coach and I got to head off to the locker room.

I wasn't all that sweaty, but I showered anyway. Coach was waiting for me when I came out with my wet hair dripping onto my dry shirt. "Shit, sorry," I said. "Do you need to lock up?"

He shook his head and just looked at me. "You're doing okay, Tyler," he said.

It was nice to hear, but it shouldn't have been something he needed to say. I shouldn't have been seeming weak or needy or insecure or whatever it was that made him think I needed to hear it. So I smiled innocently and said, "Thanks. I'm trying."

"I know you are," he said.

I turned away quickly and bent over as if there was something wrong with my shoe. It was stupid for me to react so strongly to such simple words. I guess I'd gotten a bit too used to my dad's approach, and it had left me unprepared for something softer.

"Thanks for letting me play tonight," I said once I was sure I had my voice under control. "It was fun."

"Yeah," he said quietly. "It was." Then he clapped me

on the shoulder. "Go home and get some sleep. I'll see you tomorrow."

"Yes, sir," I said. But I didn't go home right away. Instead, I stayed in the shadows by the Zamboni door and watched the next bunch of players take the ice. They were just as varied as the previous team, just as enthusiastic about getting back on the ice after a long summer off. But this time, I didn't let them see me. This time, I thought it would be better if I wasn't noticed at all.

Chapter Sixteen

- *KAREN* -

I rolled out of bed at my usual time the next day and had my running clothes on before my brain woke up enough to remember the events of the night before. The party, the girls in the bathroom, the conversation with Natalie. And on top of it all, Tyler's sweet smile, the warmth of his fingers wrapped around mine, the way he'd waded out into the lake to be sure I was okay. Damn it. I had no idea what I wanted. Or more accurately, I knew exactly what I wanted, but I wasn't sure I could have it.

But I couldn't let myself be a coward, and I didn't plan to lose the only friend I'd made since moving to town, so I headed upstairs and pulled on my running shoes. The scrapes on my arms had stiffened up overnight, and I wasn't sure I was going to be able to run all that well, but I wanted to give it a try.

I jogged carefully on my way down to the park. Tyler was already there, sitting on the ground and stretching. He saw me coming and showed me his sweet smile.

I got a few steps closer before I said, "Why didn't you tell me you'd slept with Miranda?"

It wasn't a great way to start a conversation, I guess. Tyler's smile froze, and then his expression turned serious. "It didn't seem like I should," he said cautiously. "I mean, there're lots of guys who talk about girls, but I try not to. 'Don't kiss and tell,' and all that."

"I don't understand your rules. It's okay to sleep with whoever you want, but not to mention their names?"

"Gossip," he said succinctly. When I stared at him blankly, he said, "I can't control what other people say, but I can make sure I'm not one of the ones saying it."

I nodded slowly. "Okay. Yeah. Still, a heads up would have been nice."

"I wasn't…" He shook his head impatiently, but it felt like he was frustrated with himself, not with me. "I wasn't sure what to do about that. Was it bad? Finding out about it?"

"Not terrible."

"She's still mad about it?" He didn't look guilty, exactly, but something close to it. "I thought she understood. I mean, she *said* she understood. But I guess maybe—"

"It doesn't matter," I said quickly. I didn't want to hear about his heartbreaking ways.

"You're here, at least." He peered at the bandages on my arms. "You going to be able to run with those?"

"No idea. Only one way to find out." And I started off. Tyler fell in beside me, our pace easy, and I felt my shoulders relax for the first time in too long. My arms barely hurt, and everything else felt great.

When we entered the forest, the path narrowed and we fell into single file, with me in front. I had this weird energy, making me feel like a little kid, and when we reached a fallen tree trunk I skipped up and ran along the top of it, just because I could. I glanced behind me to see Tyler following my lead, and the game was on. I leap-frogged over a boulder, ran up a hill backwards, jumped up and kicked off a wide tree trunk, and laughed as Tyler did the same. When we came out to the grassy area, I fell back and let Tyler take the lead, and the next time through the forest, he did all of my stunts and led me through a couple more.

This wasn't my usual *breathe in, thud thud, breathe out, thud thud* running. I wasn't trying to turn off my brain anymore. Instead, I felt alive, using my body for the sheer joy of it, like a little kid. I saw the grin on Tyler's face and knew he felt the same way.

Exhausted after fewer laps than usual, we threw ourselves on the grass and lay there panting like happy dogs after a long play. He rolled onto his side and grinned at me, and I smiled back at him. For a second, I thought he was going to keep rolling, bringing our sweaty bodies together, his lips finding mine...but he didn't. Instead, he said, "What are you running for? Like, are you in training for a sport?"

"No. Once I found out I wasn't going to make the Corrigan Falls Rangers, nothing else seemed worth even trying for, you know?"

"Raiders," he corrected firmly. "But, seriously, nothing but this? Just running to run?"

"Yeah. I'm not really the team-sport kind of girl."

"There are individual sports you could do."

"Like running?"

"But you don't compete, or anything?"

"I used to be a bit more focused. You know, trying to run farther, or beat my time or whatever. But now I just run."

He nodded and let his head fall back on the grass. "I like that you're athletic," he said, his eyes on the sky. "You're not watching someone else's sport, you're doing your own thing."

"I like that you're athletic, too. I mean, I'm not too crazy about the whole hockey vibe, but I guess I have to thank the team for those muscles." I was blushing even before the last syllable was out of my mouth. He rolled back onto his side to look at me, and it was my turn to stare at the clouds.

I could hear the mischievous grin in his voice when he said, "What, *these* old things? *These* muscles? You like them?" From the corner of my eye I saw him stretching his arms in an exaggeratedly casual way, flexing as if noticing them for the first time. Then he poked me gently in the ribs. "You are so *shallow*."

It had been so easy, running with him. But this, now? Flirting with him was *not* easy. I felt like I was torn in two; one part of me was excited, looking forward to what came next, but the other part was having trouble forgetting what had already happened. It probably wasn't fair, but Tyler's past was on my mind, and the knowledge made it hard for me to really enjoy the present.

He must have picked up on my hesitation, because he lay back on the grass quietly, and we both looked up at the sky for a while. Finally, he said, "There's a game Sunday afternoon. First one of the season. It's just an exhibition, no big deal, but there should be a good crowd. If you wanted… Dawn, Cooper's girlfriend? You met her last night?"

"The one with short red hair?"

"Yeah, right now. That changes pretty often. But Cooper's alternate captain of the team, and Dawn kind of looks after the social side of things for him. If you wanted, I could get you a ticket, and you could sit with her. We could do something afterward."

It would be a public announcement, I realized. Sitting with Dawn, waiting around for Tyler after the game… It'd make my role crystal clear, in the eyes of whatever hockey fans came to a pre-season game. As comforting as it would be to feel that I had a place in this town, I wasn't sure I wanted to make things clear for everyone else when they were still so unclear to me.

I guess I waited too long before speaking, because Tyler sighed. "I was right last night," he said. "I should have kept you away from all that crap. We could have kept running together, and just hung out. Now, it feels like a big deal or something, right?"

"I'd like to keep running. And hanging out…if you're okay with…" I struggled to find the words. "With that being all. You know?"

He was quiet for a while. "Just because you aren't interested, or because of my reputation?" He sat up quickly. "No, sorry, don't answer that. It doesn't matter, right?" For the first time, the smile he gave me seemed less than genuine. "Yeah, sure. We should keep running. Sure. As long as the team will let me." He stood up, his body graceful and balanced even though he was clearly in a hurry to get out of there.

"Because of me," I said quietly. He was standing in front of the sun, its rays glaring out from behind his back. It gave me a good excuse to not look directly at him. "You're great. I like you a lot, and you're really" — I waved my arm vaguely in the direction of his body — "Attractive. Obviously. But I'm kind of messed up. Everything back in Toronto, and moving here, and trying to figure out the family stuff, and starting a new school in a couple days, and honestly, it's not like I was the Queen of Stability *before* all this." I stopped for a breath. "I just don't think I can handle any other new things. Nothing big. You know?"

Tyler sank back down and sat on the grass next to me. "Yeah," he said softly. "Okay. I get it."

"I'm psycho, right?"

"You're honest. And that's a lot of shit to deal with."

"I like you. It's just not a good time."

"I like you, too. And, yeah, we should still run. Today was good for me. It was a reminder that being fit, being active… I *like* all that. It's not all about hockey. Not really." It sounded like that meant a bit more to him than it did to me, but I wasn't quite sure what and I didn't have time to figure it out because he was still talking, his voice almost apologetic. "But hanging out, that's probably going to be an added complication." He ran a hand roughly through his hair. "I know it seems weird to you, but people pay attention to me. Because of hockey. It's stupid, but we're the biggest show this town has. If you're trying to keep things quiet and give yourself some time to settle in, you might want to spare yourself the aggravation of being seen with me."

It was almost the same advice I'd gotten from Natalie the night before. It was harder to ignore it coming from

Tyler, though. And maybe he had his own reasons for not wanting a tag-along. "And I might get in the way, right? I mean, if people think we're dating, it might slow down your one-night fun."

He frowned, then shook his head. "No. It wouldn't. There're lots of girls who wouldn't care. But obviously you do. Obviously that's at least part of the reason you're not interested." He held up a hand to keep me from responding. "That's your business. I'm just saying, you should be honest about it. You can say that this is about you, but it's about me, too, right? If I was some nerdy little virgin, you wouldn't be having the same doubts."

I wasn't going to get into the whole thing with Natalie and my father. I wasn't even sure it was a good comparison; Will wasn't just a slut, he was a cheater, too, and it wasn't fair to assume Tyler would do that. But Tyler was right. I should try to be honest. So I nodded slowly and said, "I guess. Yeah, it freaks me out a bit. It's an added complication."

"I can't change the past. But if it helps, I've decided not to do that anymore. I mean, obviously if you and I were dating, I wouldn't sleep around. But even if we're not, I'm not going to. It's time to grow up. And I should be focusing on my game, anyway."

"So you wouldn't have a lot of time for a girlfriend."

"I'd make time." His voice was low, but firm.

The whole situation was too much. He was too perfect, in all but one way. I felt like someone was playing a trick on me and I'd caught on but wasn't sure who to accuse. It was my turn to stand up, and I'm sure I didn't do it as gracefully as Tyler had. "I can't do this," I said quickly. "Just running, then, if hanging out isn't a good idea. That's fine."

I started to leave, walking as quickly as I could without feeling like I was running away. But Tyler's voice stopped me. "Hey, Karen?"

I turned around and looked at him.

"It's going to be really hot this afternoon. You want to go swimming? I can't guarantee that we won't see other people, but there wouldn't be many. If you want."

"Yes." I said it without thinking, but even after my brain caught up to my mouth, I was still pleased with the answer. "I'd like that."

"I've got practice this morning, and a team dinner starting at five. But I could pick you up around one, maybe?"

"Okay." It was awkward, having him come to the house now that I knew about him and Miranda, but I wasn't going to start sneaking around. "Yeah. I'd like that. I'll see you then."

I took the long way home. I was feeling good, overall, and I wasn't looking forward to whatever new drama I'd face when I walked into the house. But mostly, I just wanted some time alone with my thoughts. I wanted to savor the way Tyler had smiled at me, and appreciate his attempts to see the situation from my perspective. And, yeah, okay, I wanted to picture the way his muscles bunched and stretched as he moved. I hadn't been joking when I said I appreciated what hockey had done for his body. It was a weird sort of balancing act, wanting so badly to be with him at the same time as knowing it was a terrible idea.

As I drew nearer the house, I felt the tension sneaking back into my shoulders even though I tried to keep them relaxed. I pushed open the back door quietly enough that I didn't disturb the occupants of the kitchen, and I stood there for a moment, watching them. The whole family was there, and they still looked perfect, sitting around the kitchen table eating their breakfasts. They were freshly scrubbed and tidily dressed, they were speaking pleasantly as they ate with impeccable table manners, and most of all, they seemed to genuinely like each other.

I must have made a sound, or maybe their hive mind just activated, because all their heads turned in my direction simultaneously. Miranda and Matt frowned, Will looked surprised, as if he'd forgotten he *had* another kid, and Natalie's head swiveled right back around to stare at Miranda as if willing her to not say something cutting.

"You want pancakes?" Sara asked cheerfully.

"I'm all sweaty. I should go shower."

No one argued. There wasn't even space for me at the table, really, not unless we all got a lot closer than anyone should get to someone coming back from a run. So I escaped down the stairs, and I could hear their conversation start up again behind me. Temporary interruption taken care of; they could go back to their perfect lives. Or at least, perfect-on-the-surface.

Chapter Seventeen

There was a scout at practice that morning. It wasn't an official thing, not this early in the season. He just happened to be in the area, he'd wanted to drop in to say hello to his old friend Coach Nichols, and, oh, there was a practice going on? Well, he might as well sit through it, since he was there.

Coach knew the system. And I wasn't exactly new to it, either. I'd been there for two years already, seen the older players given their chances to show off their skills, and now it was my turn. It was one more reason to be glad I hadn't gone back to the party the night before, for sure. I wasn't hungover, so I could do my best in practice. And I hadn't fooled around with anybody, so I hadn't felt guilty when I'd seen Karen that morning.

Even if nothing was going to happen with her, I was glad I hadn't let her down. I wanted to be the guy she wanted me to be, even if there was no real payoff for it. I wanted to be that guy for its own sake, just for my own satisfaction.

But that was *not* the shit I should be thinking about at practice, especially not with a scout in the stands. Winslow and Cooper and a few of the other older guys were in the same state I was, all nervous and trying not to show it, with the younger guys picking up on the energy and being their own kind of stupid. It was a high-energy practice, for sure. During the scrimmage at the end, I had to break up two near-fights when things got too physical and the kids didn't have enough sense to remember they were both on the same team.

I really couldn't figure out whether I'd shown the scout anything worth seeing. I'd hustled, like I always did, but maybe that was a problem right there. If I was clearly working my ass off and *still* wasn't as fast as I should be, then maybe it was clear that I just wasn't that fast. Maybe it would have been better if I'd found a way to hide how hard I was working, so it'd look like I had more in the tank and just wasn't wasting my full effort on a practice. But then I'd look like a lazy player, and nobody wanted one of those.

The whole thing was impossible to figure out and impossible to get out of my head. "Fuck it," I said, chucking a roll of stick tape into my locker with a little more force than necessary.

Winslow was beside me, as usual, and he raised an eyebrow at my little display. "You did good, Tyler." He had a weird way of speaking that always made him sound either really stoned or really wise. I tried to focus on the *wise*, this time.

"It's such a game. But they don't tell you the score until

the end."

"So just play your best, and hope for the best."

"No way, Yoda, I want to *be* the best. If I'm playing a game, I want to win." That was true. I wouldn't have made it as far as I had in hockey without being pretty damned competitive.

Winslow just grinned at me, then held one hand flat like it was a notebook and pretended to write in it with the other. "Shows good fire and intensity," he said in a serious voice. Then he forced away a grin and added, "But does not show proper respect for his teammates *or* for classic movie heroes."

"Me and Karen are going swimming this afternoon, before the team dinner," I said. I hadn't planned this and had no idea if it was a good idea, but I decided to keep going anyway. The locker room was still crowded, and I didn't want to make a public announcement so I lowered my voice a little and added, "It's supposed to be low-key. You know, not a big public event. But if you wanted to come? Maybe I could ask Cooper and Dawn, too."

"You and Karen, Cooper and Dawn…" Winslow shook his head. "Are you going to make me do it, my friend? If you guys all couple up, do I have to find a girlfriend, too? No more puck bunnies?"

"Don't call Karen my girlfriend," I warned. "Not in front of her. It's a bit weird. Probably not going to happen at all, really. So, no, I don't think you have to couple up just to be one of the team."

"Good," he said with an exaggerated sigh of relief. Then he looked at me a little more seriously. "Why isn't it going to happen? You and Karen. What's the problem?"

That wasn't an easy question to answer. Well, there was one easy answer, but it wouldn't tell the whole story, and I didn't want to get into details. So instead I said, "I just don't think I can do it, man. I can't… I can't keep denying my true feelings, you know? It's you, Winslow. It's *always* been you. No matter how hard I tried to distract myself, I couldn't do it. And I can't hide it anymore." I stood up, zipped up my jeans and then loudly said, "Chris Winslow, I love you. I have always loved you and I always will. Please, Chris, say you love me back."

Winslow had a strange expression on his face, like he wasn't sure whether to laugh or be horrified, and I knew at once that there was more to it than a reaction to my non-sense. I stared at him, and he slowly nodded behind me. I turned, and there they were—Coach, my dad, and the scout, standing in the doorway staring at me.

"He's not gay!" my dad said quickly, turning to the scout with a forced grin. "Far from it! You should see the list of bunnies he's bagged!"

I have no idea what possessed me, but I shrugged non-chalantly and looked the scout straight in the eyes as I said, "Might have been denial. Or over-compensation. Right?"

The scout nodded slowly. "Maybe," he agreed. "I know my brother slept with quite a few women before *he* came out."

In the awkward silence, I tried to figure out whether pre-tending to be in love with your best friend was homophobic. I didn't *think* so…it was the being in love *with Winslow* part that was ridiculous, not the *being gay* part. But I wasn't sure the scout with a gay brother would see it the same way. I suddenly didn't care whether he thought I was a good player or the right fit for his team, but I really didn't want him to think I was an asshole. "I hope he's happier now," I said. It was probably ridiculous, and I could see that my dad wanted me to shut up. "Your brother," I clarified.

"I think he is," the scout agreed, then turned to look at my coach. "Interesting group you've assembled here."

Coach nodded and didn't seem too worried about anything. "Some of them have character, some of them *are* characters." He rolled his eyes in my direction. "Sometimes I'm not sure which is which."

"Tyler's got a lot of character," my dad said quickly. He turned to me and said, "What was that award you won at the camp? Two years in a row he was a counselor there, and two years in a row he got the same award. What was it? Most Popular Counselor, something like that?"

"Biggest Character," I said. It wasn't true, but I was kind of enjoying seeing my dad's face turn different colors. I figured that if this scout was looking for reasons to not like me, I'd already given him a few, so there was no reason to not give him a few more.

"Biggest Pain in the Ass," my dad responded, and there was a warning tone in his voice.

I didn't want to get into a full-scale argument right there in the locker room, so I turned around to find my shirt and break the tension a little. When I turned back the scout was still watching me, though, and my dad was still watching the scout. The rest of the room was quiet, pretending to go about their business, but I could tell they were all watching, too.

"I hope you saw good things at practice," I said to the scout. I was the captain and should be acting that way. "We weren't going full-strength on the checking, obviously, but even at half-power, Winslow was knocking people around, wasn't he? You should see him in a game. Nobody gets through him. And Cooper had that sweet shot late in the scrimmage... I wish we'd had a radar gun on it to see how fast it was going."

"And you?" the scout asked with a raised eyebrow. "What did you do that should have impressed me?"

There wasn't much to say. I'd done my job and played my game, but I hadn't really shone at anything that I could think of.

"The teleportation was useful," Winslow said with a look in Cooper's direction, and Cooper nodded.

"Teleportation?" the scout asked.

Cooper was the one to answer him. "We say Mac can teleport. Because whenever there's a spot, and you say, *damn, if there was somebody in that spot I could totally make things happen*, all of a sudden, Mac's there. Coach says it's because he's smart and can read how the play is going to go and get himself in position, but Winslow and me...we know Mac's not all that smart. So we figure he must be able to teleport."

The scout nodded. Then he grinned in Winslow's direction and held up his hand like a notepad, using his other to write imaginary notes, making it clear just how long he'd been eavesdropping on our locker room conversation. "Shows good sense of teamwork and comradeship," he said seriously, then added, "May not be totally in touch with reality as we know it."

They left, then, my dad looking like he wasn't sure whether to be pleased or pissed off. I turned around and flopped down on the bench by my locker. It should have been nice to hear my teammates saying those things about me, but really it just made me feel more nervous, like they were building an even higher pedestal for me to fall off. "That was one scout on a fucking preliminary visit. We're supposed to be able to keep this up for a full season?"

"It's all part of the test," Winslow said, clapping me on the shoulder. "They want to see how we can handle pressure."

"Or they just get their kicks out of torturing us," Cooper said.

Suddenly, I really wanted to get out of there. "You and Dawn want to go swimming?" I asked Cooper. "Winslow doesn't want to be the third wheel, but he'd probably be okay with being the fifth."

"Sounds good. I'll give Dawn a call. If she can't make it, Winslow can be my date." Cooper smiled in his direction. "Mac's not the only one who's got his eye on you, sweetheart."

"It's nice to be wanted," Winslow said blandly.

I wasn't really listening anymore. I wanted to get the hell out of there and go pick Karen up. So I did. We went down to the lake, and it wasn't long before the others joined us. Dawn and Karen seemed to get along, and they led the conversation to places it would never have gone if it was just us guys. That is, we talked about things other than hockey. It was a good afternoon, and I knew I wasn't the only one who wished we could stay at the lake instead of going back in and getting ready for dinner.

But it was the first team dinner of the year, and it wouldn't look good if both captains blew it off. Winslow probably could have escaped if he'd tried, but his whole family had come up for it and they wouldn't have been impressed. So we took a final dip and headed back to the cars, the sun and the wind drying us as we walked.

It had been a good afternoon, and it would have felt totally natural to stick around a bit after the other cars had left, would have felt right to lean Karen up against the side of the truck and kiss her. Nothing more than that, probably, just…just making out a bit. Making it clear that I wanted there to be something more between us, without pressuring her to decide exactly what that should look like.

Yeah, that would have felt natural, but it was almost certainly against the rules. So we climbed into the truck and drove back into town. I knew Karen's skin would be warm from the sun and smell like the lake, and I had to pretend I wasn't thinking about any of that. It felt like just one more game I was playing, one more lie I was telling to the world. I was the only one who knew the truth, and I was pretty sure that if I tried to tell anyone else about it, they'd just want me to shut up. So I kept quiet, and I smiled when Karen wanted me to. It was the best I could think to do.

Chapter Eighteen

- *KAREN* -

This time when Tyler pulled up outside the house to drop me off after our swim, there was no crowd of family members in the front yard, but I still felt awkward. It had been a great afternoon. We'd gotten along well, we'd had fun. There had been several times that I'd wanted him to kiss me, and I definitely felt like he returned the interest, but he hadn't made a move. And now, sitting in his truck, it seemed like another natural time for us to slide closer together and let our bodies do what they wanted. But instead of letting any of that happen, or *making* any of it happen, I just gave him a small smile and slid out of my seat. "Thanks," I said. "That was fun."

He nodded. "Yeah. I'll give you a call, okay? Or you can call me. Or I'll see you at school on Tuesday. Something."

So many options, but I still felt like I didn't have any

choice in the matter. I'd see him, sure, but I was too weak to trust myself to really take advantage of it. "Okay," I said, and I headed toward the house. I thought about the first day of school, and how maybe I'd see him walking down the hall with another girl, smiling at her in his sweet way, and I knew I'd have nothing to complain about, nothing to reproach him with.

I was feeling almost queasy as I made my way around the back of the house and toward the kitchen door. I'd apparently decided that the front door was off limits, and now it always seemed like I was sneaking around. One more weird, pointless decision on my part.

My random angst turned into full-blown anxiety when I walked into the kitchen and saw Natalie standing at the counter, her hands gripping the edges of the sink as if she were trying to keep herself from being blown away in a tornado. Will was a few feet behind her, his expression strained.

He turned to look at me, but she didn't. Somehow, I knew too much. I knew she wasn't looking at me because if she did I'd see that she was crying. I knew that he was the one who'd made her cry. Probably cheating, but it didn't really matter. He looked guilty and almost shocked. I could see him trying to work up to being indignant, as if her reaction was out of line, as if she should have just shrugged off whatever his current transgression was.

Will was my father, but I wanted to go over and give Natalie a hug, maybe even kiss her cheek and whisper some words of comfort. Instead, I turned my head and found my way down to the basement.

Surprise number two. All three kids were down there in the rec room, huddled on the big leather sofa with their faces tense. Matt was at one end looking concerned, and Sara and Miranda were cuddled up together at the other end. Their saccharine-sweet "we all love and support each other" bullshit should have made me nauseated, but it didn't.

I had no idea what to say, so I headed into my bedroom and shut the door. I didn't know if this was typical, just another fight in a stormy marriage, or if it was something bigger than that. The kids didn't seem to be taking it too well, and that wasn't a good sign.

How much of this was my fault? I hadn't exactly been a ray of sunshine since I'd arrived. Well, that was a bit of an understatement. I'd been a nightmare for the entire family, an unwelcome reminder of Will's past misbehavior who refused to shut up and let things settle down. Miranda was a bitch, no doubt, but I hadn't been much better, and it had been Natalie who'd been stuck between the two of us.

I was tempted to go back out to the rec room. I could sit on the floor, not presuming to be part of their little club but still close enough to draw a bit of comfort. Maybe I'd lean back against the sofa and somebody would put their hand on my shoulder.

Or maybe Miranda would kick me in the kidneys and then start screaming at me to go back to where I came from and get out of their perfect lives.

Not a chance I was willing to take, so I lay down on my bed and stared at the ceiling, instead.

When I finally emerged from my cave and made my way upstairs, Natalie was gone. I hadn't heard a thing. No yelling, no slammed doors, no crying. Either the house was even more soundproof than I'd thought, or Natalie had left with her typical dignity and poise.

Will was on the phone, ordering pizza, and the kids were sitting at the kitchen table looking shell-shocked.

Will hung up and smiled at me. For the first time, I saw desperation in his attempted charm. "Natalie's mom isn't feeling too well, so Natalie's going to stay over there for a couple days, help nurse her back to health. We get to look after ourselves for a bit." He was trying to make it sound like a fun adventure, but no one else even cracked a smile. Still, he kept going. "Pizza for breakfast, lunch, and dinner, if we want!"

As if Natalie's only contribution to the family was her cooking.

Sara had clearly been crying, and it looked like she was ready to start again. "But I *don't* want," she said plaintively.

"Pizza's your favorite!" Will reached out to muss Sara's hair, but she jerked away and eyed him reproachfully.

"She's coming back, right?" Sara stared at Will as if trying to read the truth from his soul. "A couple days. That's all, right?"

"Probably not even that long," Will scoffed. "Grandma Patterson is tough. She'll be on her feet in no time, and Natalie will be right back where she belongs. Everything will be normal again." He might have been convincing himself, but I don't think anyone else in the room believed him.

None of the kids even looked at me, and it had never been more painfully clear that I was an outsider. I felt awkward, sure, but that was all. I had never really been a part of the family, so it wasn't all that horrible for me to see it being torn apart.

Except that somehow, it was.

I had never thought I wanted this family, never thought I

needed them. *I'd* been the one pulling away and telling them to give me space. Now, though, I realized that I *did* need them. Natalie, at least, but even the others meant something. For all his failings, Will was the only real relative I had left. Sara was a sweetheart, both younger and older than her years. Matt and Miranda…well, Matt and Miranda were a challenge, but I definitely envied their closeness and the way they seemed to really enjoy spending time with each other. This was family worth fighting for. Worth saving.

"We should have a salad," I said. "Shouldn't we?" Natalie was a big fan of fresh vegetables at every meal. "Sara, can you help me make a salad?" I knew the next part was a gamble, but I went for it. "And, Matt, you made that dressing the other night, right? The pesto vinaigrette? Do we have the ingredients for you to make that again?"

For an awkward moment, nobody moved. I was about to slink away back to my cave when help came from the most unexpected source. "Yeah," Miranda said decisively. "Matt, that dressing was great. Sara, can you go pick us some tomatoes and cucumbers?" She stood up, tall and graceful, and moved toward the cupboards. "I'll set the table, Karen, if you can figure out the rest of the salad stuff?" It sounded genuine, like a polite invitation to share a project, not an order or a trap.

Still, I was suspicious. "Okay," I said cautiously. There was no punch line, no sarcastic response from Miranda. We all just started our assigned tasks, while Will stood with his back to the counter, watching us work. It was kind of amazing how smoothly everything went. We made the salad, the pizza arrived, and we all sat down to eat. With nothing to keep ourselves distracted, the lack of conversation was a little more obvious than it had been while we were working, but we were able to pretend that we were just not talking with our mouths full.

We were just finishing up the meal when the phone rang, and Sara jumped out of her chair as if she'd been given a shock. "I'll get it," she yelled, sprinting for the kitchen.

We could all hear her answer the phone and start sobbing. "Why are you gone? When are you coming back? You're coming back, right? Can you come back *now*?"

Will had the grace to look ashamed. He stood abruptly and said, "You guys take care of cleanup, okay? And…take care of Sara." He left us, then, striding off toward the den.

Miranda sighed in disgust and growled, "This is all your fault."

I couldn't disagree. I couldn't even look at her.

I was a bit surprised to hear Matt say, "Come on, Miranda." He didn't sound like he was defending me. It was more like he was defending himself, and when I made myself look at Miranda, she was staring at him, not me.

"*Your* fault," she repeated. "That's what set her off."

I was completely confused. It felt like a conversation I shouldn't be hearing, but it would feel too awkward to stand up and leave. Besides, I was curious. What had Matt done?

"It has nothing to do with any of you. I can't believe Beth even mentioned it." Beth was his girlfriend; I hadn't met her because she'd spent her summer as a camp counselor somewhere up north and had just gotten back recently. But what the hell had she said that could set off something like this?

Miranda whirled toward me, and suddenly I was no longer the fly on the wall for this conversation. "He was cheating on her," she announced angrily.

I had no idea what to say. "Yeah. I thought…I thought everybody knew that?"

It was her turn to look confused, but her expression quickly changed to disgust. "Not Daddy! Matt! Beth was away for the summer, and Matt was going out with Andrea Davis! Sneaking around, not telling anybody." She snarled at her twin. "Just like Daddy! God, Matt, is it honestly that hard to just control yourself?"

"You're one to talk," he fired back. "You gave it up for Tyler MacDonald without much self-control, didn't you?"

This was too much. I'd have thought I'd love to see them at each other's throats, but it turned out it was kind of sad. And almost scary. "Shhh," I hissed. "Sara's in the kitchen. She's already freaking out, she doesn't need to be worrying about you guys, too!"

They both stared at me, and I could see the snarky response just ready to fly out of Miranda's mouth. Instead, she closed her lips tightly and spoke much more quietly when she told Matt, "You need to make this better."

"How?" he replied in a hoarse whisper. "It doesn't even make sense. Why would she leave Dad because *I* did something stupid?"

"You're admitting it was stupid, at least?" Miranda sounded slightly mollified.

"Yeah," he said, "I guess. I mean, I really like them both…"

"You're a pig!" Miranda snarled.

"Okay," I interrupted. "Maybe that should be a conversation you guys have some time when Sara isn't quite so close."

And of course, that was when Sara appeared in the doorway. "I'm not a little kid!" she yelled. It was the first time she'd been upset with me, and I didn't like it. "I don't want to be lied to, and I don't want people hiding things from me!"

"Is Mom still on the phone?" Miranda interrupted. "I need to talk to her."

"She said she was staying at Grandma and Grandpa's for a couple days. She said we can call her there whenever we need to." Sara sounded a little calmer now that she had news to share.

"I need to talk to her now," Miranda said firmly. She looked at her brother. "And so do you. We need to fix this."

She stalked off toward the stairs, her brother following reluctantly, and Sara looked at me, then turned away. "I'm going to watch TV," she announced, and headed for the basement.

I was left in the dining room looking at the remains of the dinner. Will had asked us to tidy up, but we'd been the ones who'd *made* the dinner. Well, us and the pizza place. Still, it didn't seem like my job to be the family's maid. I pushed my chair back and felt in my pocket to be sure my cell was there. I wanted to make a call of my own, and I didn't feel like putting it off until after I'd done the dishes. It didn't matter what accusations Miranda was throwing around; this whole situation was Will's fault. He should clean up his own mess, in the kitchen and elsewhere.

I felt like everything was spinning around me, shifting and changing too fast too keep up with. The only time I felt stable was when I was with Tyler. Maybe it was a mistake, and maybe I was setting myself up for the same sort of pain Natalie was suffering from. But I needed to feel safe, and I knew Tyler could give me that.

Chapter Nineteen

- TYLER -

"I have no idea what that little show in the locker room was about, but in the future you will keep your goddamned mouth *shut* when there is a scout around." My dad was doing a weird thing where he tried to look like he was smiling and happy at the same time that he was cussing me out. He wasn't very good at it and probably anyone who saw him would just think he had a weird facial tick or something. They'd definitely realize that he was giving me shit. But we were at a team dinner, around guys who'd seen me and my dad interact for years now. They'd know he was giving me shit just because they saw that his lips were moving.

"I didn't know there was a scout around," I said defensively. "He was spying on us or something."

"You were in the goddamn locker room," my dad growled. "From now on, you treat that as a public space. No, you treat it like it's a goddamn boardroom you've been brought to for a big interview. You should *always* be on your best behavior, *always* trying to impress people. There is no god-damn room for mistakes here, Tyler."

"Was he pissed off? The guy this afternoon. He seemed okay when he left." I wasn't trying to defend myself anymore, just trying to figure out whether I *had* been homophobic or offensive. Not that the scout was the final word or anything, but I didn't really know anyone who was openly gay, so he was the best judge I had.

"I don't know," my dad said disgustedly. "He was hard to read. And, really, it's not like you want to get drafted by Ottawa anyway. We're looking for a big market team for you, Tyler, somewhere you can use that pretty face to earn yourself some serious endorsement money."

Between his bragging about my puck bunnies earlier in the day and calling me pretty at night, I was hitting a limit for how gross my dad could get without me puking on him. "Okay, well, I'll try to keep an eye out for scouts in the future," I said. And I began to understand what my grandma had meant when she'd said I was born with a devil on my shoulder. For some reason I felt compelled to add, "And I'll try to keep my feelings for Winslow under cover. Not liter-ally. Well, maybe literally, if he actually comes to his senses and realizes that our love is meant to be."

"What the hell is wrong with you?" my dad asked. It sounded like a genuine question, but I didn't really have an answer for him. Then he made it worse. "Is this about the new girl? What's her name? The one I'm hearing you're spending so much time with. You do not have time for a seri-ous girlfriend, Tyler. You want to screw around and sow your wild oats, that's just fine. You need to be sure you don't get anyone knocked up, because that is *not* a headache we want to be dealing with, but other than that, go for it. But keep your head in the game. No distractions."

Yeah, getting permission from my dad to sleep around? That was the hat trick of gross dad comments, and definitely more creepiness than I could handle in one day. "I should go," I said. We'd already eaten dinner and done all the cheesy toasts and all the rest of the crap that apparently made The Corrigan Falls Raiders into the best darn OHL team ever, so I could escape if I needed to. And it was definitely time. "There are puck bunnies out there just *begging* to have totally non-distracting sex with me. I can't disappoint them."

"You didn't used to be so mouthy," my dad said. He sounded almost sad, but as always there was a distinctly angry undertone.

"I used to be a little kid," I reminded him. "You've known me since before I could speak. It'd be kind of amazing if I hadn't changed at all in that time, wouldn't it?"

"You weren't this mouthy *two weeks* ago," he said.

I didn't answer him, but I was pretty sure he was actually telling the truth. It wasn't just Karen. Well, yeah, it was probably mostly her. But not in the obvious way. Not, like, she was mouthy so I was, too. It was more like she thought about things and tried to point out when they didn't make sense, and I was trying to do the same, and that made both of us—well, it made both of us a little mouthy, maybe. It wasn't an accusation I was going to lose a lot of sleep over.

My phone rang then and I was happy to answer it, even happier when I saw the name on the call display. I knew my dad was standing there, listening and judging, but I tried not to let myself care. I needed a break. "Hey," I said.

"Can you come get me?" Karen asked. I waited for more details, but she didn't offer any.

"You're at home?"

"If that's what you want to call it," she agreed.

"Okay. Give me ten minutes." I hung up and looked at my father. "I'll be at the rink on time or early, every day. I'll work my ass off, and I'll try to be a leader. I'll play the best hockey I can. That's all I can do."

He shook his head disgustedly. "If you throw this chance away, you're going to spend the rest of your life regretting it. Trust me on that."

He said it like he'd been a prospect himself. He always talked that way, but I'd looked him up, and he'd never even made the OHL. A year and a half in Junior A, and that was it. He'd never got too specific about this mythical chance he'd thrown away, but looking at his dates in the league and my birth date, it wasn't too hard to figure out what he was talking about. Bullshit, of course, because a nineteen-year-old still in Junior A does *not* make it to the big league, whether or not a baby comes along to slow him down, but I guess it's what he told himself to make his life easier to accept. And it gave him a good way to try to guilt me. It had worked for a while, before I understood how the hockey system worked.

But now, I just nodded and let his words flow over me. "I won't throw anything away," I said. "But I need to go."

He didn't try to stop me. But I knew he was standing there, watching me leave, and I knew he wished I was different than I was. Just like I wished the same thing for him. Neither one of us was going to get our wish, though, so it was up to both of us to just try to get along as best we could with the family we were stuck with.

Chapter Twenty

- *KAREN* -

I was waiting on the front steps when Tyler's truck rolled up in front of the house. He'd sounded weird and tense on the phone, and I'd had a moment's doubt about dragging him away from whatever he was doing, but his answer had seemed sincere enough. "Give me ten minutes," he'd said.

He made it to the house in five, and I practically ran over the lawn to climb into the truck after he pushed the door open for me. "You okay?" he asked. When I didn't answer right away, he asked, "You have somewhere you want to go?"

"Anywhere. I want…anywhere."

He didn't ask any more questions, just pulled away from the curb and drove. The night air was still warm, and we drove with the windows down, out of town and into the darkness of a summer night in the country.

I wasn't surprised when we pulled off the highway onto

the increasingly familiar dirt road leading to our beach. It felt different at night, though. The headlights cut through the darkness, but when we pulled into the grassy parking area and Tyler turned the engine off, everything was dark. I could barely see him, and that actually made things easier.

I unbuckled my seatbelt and slid across the bench seat toward him. I'd hoped my closeness would be enough of a hint, but he didn't move, so I took a deep breath and twisted around a little, bringing my left hand to his shoulder and resting my right on his thigh.

"What are you doing, Karen?"

"I must not be doing a very good job, if you can't tell."

"Yeah, okay, I think I can tell, but…why? I thought you didn't want—"

My finger on his lips stopped his talking. "I changed my mind," I whispered. I wanted to shut my brain off, wanted to stop telling myself everything was my fault. I wanted to stop trying to control things that couldn't be controlled. Natalie had followed the rules, and look what it had gotten her.

I squirmed up onto my knees, then threw my right leg across his lap so I was wedged between his chest and the steering wheel. It was a good thing he had long legs or there wouldn't have been room, especially since he wasn't exactly contorting himself to make any of this easier. I froze at the thought. "Did you change your mind, too? You don't want this anymore?"

He didn't answer right away, and I was just about to launch myself back to my own side of the truck when I felt his hands come to rest gently on my hips. "I want it. You. I want you. I just don't… What's going on? Are you okay?"

I didn't want to talk, so I leaned forward enough to find

his lips with mine. He was hesitant at first, and it was kind of a rush to feel like the aggressor, like *I* was the one with all the experience who knew what she was doing. But it didn't take long for him to get warmed up and get into it, and that was a whole different kind of rush, because damn it, the boy could kiss! His lips were warm and soft, his tongue firm but not invasive. His hands didn't go anywhere too serious, but they ran over my head, my arms, my back, my legs with just the right amount of pressure. It felt like he was kissing my whole body, even though his lips barely left mine.

I was out of breath and almost trembling from adrenaline, but I wanted more. I wanted to turn my brain off more completely, and I wanted to feel even more connected. Less alone. I stuck my scabbed elbows out to the sides and brought my hands up to Tyler's chest, where I found something other than his usual T-shirt. "Is this a tie? Are you wearing a tie?"

"I came from a team dinner." He sounded a little out of breath himself, but now that my voice had broken the spell, he lifted his hands to my shoulders and held my body away from his. "What's going on? I mean, if you want this, if you're sure…that's excellent. But I need to know what changed. I need to be sure you're sure."

"*I* changed," I said almost fiercely. "I got tired of doing the smart thing all the time and trying to be careful. People still get hurt, even if they're doing everything right."

"If you're looking for someone to do stupid things with you, you've found the right guy. But, seriously, this seems like it should probably be a conversation—"

This time I shut him up by running my hands down his chest and to the waistband of his dress pants. I had no idea where I got so brazen; I felt like I was drunk, or high, but really I guess I was just fed up. "I don't think it should. No conversation." No thinking, just feeling. I kissed him while I worked up my courage, then said, "Do you have a condom?"

He pulled his face away from mine and drew a deep, ragged breath, almost a gasp. "Seriously, Karen, I can't keep being the good guy, here. Are you sure about this? Really sure?"

I wasn't sure, really, but I kissed him anyway and tried to look confident. "Yeah. I want to."

Things changed pretty quickly after that. Once he was convinced that I was serious, Tyler got serious, too. The easy way he pulled a rolled up blanket from behind the seat and fished a condom out of the glove box showed that he was practiced at all this. He spread the blanket on the grass and our clothes disappeared like magic, almost too fast, leaving me strangely disoriented. Then I remembered that I was *trying* to feel that way, trying to shut my brain off and let things happen. It would have been easier if I'd had something to drink, maybe.

My focus was clearly somewhere else, because it took me longer than it should have to realize that Tyler had stopped everything. I frowned at him. "What?"

He shook his head. "Okay, one more time...this is what you want?" Somehow, his sweet little-boy smile didn't seem inappropriate, even when it was attached to a naked body I was still too shy to truly look at. "Because if you stop me now, I'm gonna be a bit frustrated. But if you stop me after this point, I'm really gonna be *pissed*."

It didn't sound like a threat. Instead, it was a reminder that as angry as he might be, he'd still stop if I told him to. Knowing that helped me relax. "No. I'm not going to change my mind. But...slow down a little, okay?"

And he did. His actions felt a little less polished at the slower speed, and I liked that. Before, I'd felt like my body was an equation he was trying to solve, a machine he wanted to fix; I had to admit he was a pretty skilled mathematician or mechanic or whatever, but it seemed impersonal. Once he slowed down, though, I felt like it was *me* that he was touching, and he seemed to know some tricks about my body that I hadn't even figured out yet. Even though he'd said he'd be pissed if we had to stop, he still kept checking in with me to make sure I was happy with where things were going. And every time he checked in, it made me more sure. I'd started this because I was upset, but every time he paused, every questioning look or gentle, murmured "Okay?" made me realize that I wasn't upset anymore. I wasn't with Tyler because I wanted to forget; I was with him because I wanted to do something worth remembering.

Everything was in contrast to something else. His hands were gentle, but their skin was calloused and rough. The night air was cool, but his body was warm. His strength made me feel weak, but when I touched him and I saw how he reacted, I knew I was powerful. And as we moved together, I felt anchored to him, solid and strong, at the same time as I seemed to be soaring and flying.

When things finally wound down, I felt good about it all. It had been unplanned, that was for sure, but we'd been careful, and I really liked him. And lying there on the soft blanket, our limbs entwined, looking up at the stars… I felt peaceful and good.

For about three minutes; then, my brain turned back on.

"How was your dinner?" I asked. "I'm sorry if I dragged you away from it."

"I'd much rather be here," he said as he kissed the top of my head. The words were sweet, but there was something bitter in his tone.

I squirmed around a little so I could get a better look at his face. "Was it not fun? Like, boring, or…?"

"It was the parents' dinner," he said, as if that explained something. I just stared at him blankly. "My mom couldn't make it, but my dad came."

"And you and your dad don't get along?"

He was quiet for too long.

"Natalie left," I said abruptly. "Will's wife. My step-mother. I don't know for how long. I don't really know why, except…I think it's because of the cheating."

He nodded slowly. "I wonder what took her so long."

That was an interesting perspective. Actually, it was a logical, normal perspective. It was how I would have felt a couple weeks earlier, before I'd gotten used to the family's Don't Ask Don't Tell policy on paternal infidelity. I needed to think about that, but I didn't want to do it right then. "Besides your dad, was the dinner okay?"

Another long silence, and I was just about to break it again when he said, "There *is* no 'besides my dad' when it comes to me and hockey. If he's there, he's all over me. All over the coaches, the support staff, the other players' dads. It's kind of out of control." He sounded resigned.

I'd been so wrapped up in my own misery that I'd sort of forgotten that other people might have problems, too. "You said your family live up in Huntsville, didn't you? How often does your dad come down?"

"During hockey season? Every game, and most practices. He pretty much lives here."

"He doesn't work?"

"Got laid off a couple years ago. Now he says his job is getting me to the NHL." Tyler shook his head as if clearing out unpleasantness, and when he stilled I kissed him. He seemed happy to be distracted.

We stayed there together until we got cold and had to get dressed, and then we sat in the truck for a while, not driving or even talking. Finally, Tyler said, "My dad wants me to stop running. Wants me to stop seeing you, too."

I was dressed warmly by then, but I still felt chilled. "Why?"

"He doesn't want me distracted." He shrugged. "Or he doesn't want me out of his control. It's hard to be sure which. Both, I guess." He looked over at me and smiled. "Doesn't matter. He doesn't get to decide *everything* for me. He doesn't get to decide that." He reached over and wrapped his fingers around mine.

"I was going to ask if it was too late to get a ticket to the game tomorrow," I said. "But maybe it'd be better to keep this a bit quiet."

"No," he said firmly. "It's not better. At least not for me. If you want to come, I can get you a ticket. Absolutely."

"You're playing London, right?" He looked at me in surprise, and I grinned. "I looked it up."

"I thought you didn't care about hockey." He was kind of digging for the compliment, but I didn't mind giving it to him anyway.

"I still don't care about hockey. But I'm starting to take a bit of an interest in a certain player. I hear he's really good. Captain of the team, leading scorer. Nice muscles, killer smile."

"Sounds like it'd be worth your time to go see him,"

Tyler agreed. "Maybe if you play your cards right, he'll ask you to do something after the game."

"I can only dream about such a privilege."

"Monday's a big team day. We have to go to a bunch of public events and act like big shots. It's brutal. And then school starts on Tuesday. I have a ten o'clock curfew from then on. Not on Saturdays, unless there's a Sunday game, but we travel a lot on the weekends."

I nodded slowly, then braced myself. "So, what are you saying? This was a summer thing, and you're too busy during the year?"

"What?" He turned fast, his face genuinely confused. "No. I just… I don't know. I guess *this* part of things—cutting out whenever we feel like it, swimming all day, having fun—that's a summer thing, yeah. But spending time with you? No, that's not something I plan to give up. Not unless you make me."

Well, that was pretty much exactly the right answer. I wanted to kiss him, but I guess I'd used up all my brazenness on my earlier display so I just squeezed his fingers. He was the one who tugged gently on my hand, pulling me over so our lips could meet in the middle.

I was really glad I'd called Tyler. Sure, it wasn't what I'd planned, and I'd jumped about fifty steps ahead of where I should be if I was following the regular relationship rules, but I didn't care. Tyler and I could make our *own* rules, and the first one, as far as I was concerned, was that we should ignore what anyone else thought was right and do what we knew was good for *us*.

The kiss got more heated, and I didn't do a thing to stop it or slow anything down. I liked Tyler's body, and I liked the way he made me feel, and I didn't see any reason to keep myself from enjoying those things. Then I thought of Miranda, and all the other girls, and I wondered if Tyler had done all the same things with them. Probably even in this very truck, maybe even parked in the same place. It was all special for me, but for Tyler it was just routine.

He obviously felt my body react to my thoughts and he pulled away and looked at me quizzically. "You okay?" he asked.

"How many other girls have you brought here?" I asked. Then I quickly said, "No, sorry, that was a stupid thing to ask. I don't want to know."

He pulled even farther away, all the way back to his own side of the bench seat. Not quite what I'd had in mind. "None," he said slowly. "Not here." He shrugged as if he knew that was only addressing a detail of the problem, not the overall issue. "I can't do anything about that. About the past. But I've never asked a girl to come to a game before. They've asked me, and I've gotten tickets for them some-times but I never... I never *wanted* them there. Not like I want you to be there." He looked at me as if trying to judge whether his words were making me feel better.

"Okay," I said. It wasn't ideal, but he was right—there was nothing he could do about it. So I forced myself to smile. "You're pretty close to perfect in a lot of other ways, so I guess it wouldn't be fair if there wasn't at least one thing that I wasn't crazy about."

He smiled in return, but he looked tired. And he didn't move back over to my side of the truck. "Do you need to get home?" he asked.

But I didn't want to leave it like that, with me insecure and him sad and frustrated. "Can we swim?"

"It's kind of cold out…"

"So the water will feel warm." I didn't push, though.

Finally, he nodded. "Yeah. Okay."

He pushed his door open and climbed out, then looked back inside to see why I wasn't moving yet. With the light from the ceiling shining down on me, I reached out and pulled the glove box open, then tried to look confident and in control as I felt inside and pulled out a condom. He was watching me like I was a kitten performing a surprising trick, but when I held the foil packet up for his inspection, he grinned at me. "More than just swimming?"

"Maybe," I said, still trying to sound sophisticated about it all. "Good to be prepared."

"Absolutely," he said, and I could see a little heat flaring behind the amusement in his eyes.

So we followed our trail down to the beach and we swam, the water as warm as I'd predicted against the cool evening air. When we were out deep, nothing around us but the dark lake and the star-sprinkled sky, I cupped my hands and scooped up some water, then let it dribble gently over Tyler's head. He sputtered a little when it hit his face, but he didn't move away, and I did it a few more times. "What are you up to?" he finally asked.

"I'm washing them away. You're clean, now. Just you and me." For good measure, I sent a handful down over my own face as well, and said, "See? We're good. Both of us."

"That easy?" He sounded like he was willing to be convinced.

I nodded. "Yeah. That easy."

And right then, right there, it really was.

Chapter Twenty-One

- TYLER -

The game went well. It was only an exhibition so it really didn't count for anything, but we gave our rookies a lot of ice time and most of them rose to the challenge. Those that didn't…well, the coaches still had some cuts to make, so it was good for them see how the guys did under pressure.

I didn't get a lot of playing time, just enough to make sure I had my feet under me and a little more when the coach thought the rookies needed some on-ice leadership. Coach had Christiansen, the rookie center who might be my replacement, playing left wing with me, and I set him up for a pretty sweet goal. When I saw his name on the scoreboard, it felt like I'd cut my own throat by making my competition look good, but there wasn't any way around it. Hockey was a team sport, and Christiansen was on my team.

Karen and I went out afterward, down to the lake for

a bit and then into town for dinner with some of the guys. It was weird to be with her in a group. I kept wanting to stop the conversation to make sure everybody had noticed what a cool thing she'd just said or done. It wasn't because I was insecure or worried that they wouldn't like her. I just wanted to have someone to share it all with, like that burst of excitement you get when you meet someone who likes the same obscure band or has the same favorite movie. I guess I was a Karen fan, and I wanted to start a fan club.

I managed to keep myself under control, though. And Monday was as stupid as I'd known it would be, all of the guys from the team acting like we were big shots, signing autographs and getting our pictures taken with people and talking like we actually knew a damn thing about anything. The people who came to see us were grown men acting like little kids, grown women acting like...well, acting like that name I wasn't supposed to be calling people anymore. I called Karen a few times, whenever I got the chance, and she laughed at me and teased me back into being a good sport about it all.

That lasted until we hit our last stop. It was a community barbecue, with grilled chicken, ribs, corn, and homemade pies, so we were all looking forward to it. Winslow always got off on these events, even without the food, and he was practically dancing as he jumped off the bus in front of me. Then he stopped, turned, and quietly said, "Sorry, man."

I had no idea what he was talking about until I looked in the direction he'd been facing before he turned, and I saw my dad standing there with his arm around the shoulders of a guy holding an expensive-looking camera. Shit. He'd said he was going home for a couple days after the team-family dinner, but I guess he'd changed his mind, or at least come back early. He smiled in my direction, waved happily, and then there was a blur of movement near me and I was being tackled around the middle by Trina, my little sister. She was almost fifteen but usually acted a lot younger, which was just fine by me. My brother Travis was standing a few feet away, his adolescent dignity keeping him from a similar display but his smile wide and genuine.

"Hey, guys!" I said, returning Trina's hug and grinning in Travis's direction. I'd been up for a weekend visit at the start of the summer, but that had been it since Christmas. I was surprised by how good it was to see them.

"Hey, bigshot," Travis said, punching my arm. I moved fast, grabbing him around the shoulders while still holding on to Trina with my other arm, and I pulled Travis in for a half-second of pure kid-bonding-time. He backed away fast, but he was still smiling, and he kept close by as our mom walked toward us.

"Baby," she said, brushing my cheek with her fingers like she always did when she first saw me. "You grew."

"Not enough," I said shortly, trying not to look in my dad's direction. "But I've been eating my vegetables."

"You hear that, Travis?" she said, frowning playfully in his direction. "Athletes need to care about nutrition."

I felt like I should say something. I mean, a mom nagging her kid to eat right wasn't exactly new, but it was kind of sad to see them using hockey as their big parenting goal post for the second time around. But I didn't want to ruin the big family reunion with a heavy discussion, so I said, "How 'bout you, Trina? You eating your vegetables? Going to grow up big and strong?"

"Thin and graceful," my mom corrected. "Vegetables are important for that, too. But Trina isn't the one who wants to eat pizza for three meals a day."

"Pizza does have vegetables on it," Travis said, and then Dad arrived with the photographer.

"We got some great shots," he said happily. "It's important to sell hockey as a game for the whole family; teams want players who understand that."

"Did he hire you or kidnap you?" I asked the photographer.

"I'm here to cover the event for the Corrigan Falls Examiner," he replied and extended his hand. "Dave Conway. I'm new."

"Yeah, I didn't think I recognized you. You do community stuff, or are you the guy covering the team now?" I could see that my dad was pleased with my interest, but I wasn't asking for myself. Getting good press coverage was good for the team, and it was part of my job to make sure the reporters liked us.

"Just the community side of things. Amanda Shears is still covering the sports beat."

I'd slept with Amanda Shears after the third and fourth games of our first playoff series the year before. Didn't seem wise to mention that right then.

I saw the team's public relations manager looking impatiently in my direction and said, "I have to go do some stuff, but we're supposed to be eating here. Can I come find you guys in a bit?"

They agreed, and I went off to try to seem modest yet confident, mature yet enthusiastic while talking to an endless stream of hockey fans. My dad was trailing along behind the photographer, making sure he got shots of me in as many poses as possible. I felt bad for the guy, but at least it was keeping my dad off my back.

When we finally sat down to eat, I got sandwiched in between Travis and Trina for a few more pictures, but the photographer finally escaped my dad's clutches and we all just ate like a more or less normal family. It was after dinner that things got bad.

My dad sent Trina and Travis off to bring him some paperwork from the car, and then he and my mom drew me down to a far end of the barbecue. "You're turning eighteen in a couple weeks," my dad said. It wasn't exactly news, so I waited for him to get to the point. "Legally an adult. Able to enter into binding contracts. Pretty exciting time, isn't it?"

"Yeah, I've been really, really looking forward to entering into some binding contracts."

My mom frowned at me in disapproval. As always, she seemed vaguely embarrassed by my dad but didn't want anyone else to be disrespectful.

My dad just forced a smile, and that was when I knew he was building up to something big. If he wasn't yelling at me, he must really want something. But of course he couldn't just come out and ask for it. "This family has sacrificed a lot for your career, Tyler." He held up his hand as if to silence me, but I hadn't been planning on arguing. "Of course we did it out of love. We don't expect to be repaid. But the fact is, it's been expensive. I had to take time off work in order to help out, I have to pay for somewhere to stay when I'm down here, there's meals, gas for traveling back and forth…" He shrugged. "Expenses. Lots of them."

"We could probably cut down on some of that," I

tried, but that wasn't what he was looking for from the conversation.

"We knew it was important, so we made it work," he said. "But it's taken its toll."

I looked at my mom, but she wasn't giving me the punch line. "What toll?" I asked.

"We're in some pretty serious financial trouble," my dad said carefully. "We've built up a lot of debt. We thought we could get by until next year, but it's not looking too good right now."

Next year. By then, in his deluded mind, I'd be in the NHL for sure, making the big bucks, and I could pay them back for everything they'd sacrificed. The plan was clear and not exactly surprising; I'd known he expected to get a serious payout if I hit the big time. But I wasn't sure about the new twist. "What do you mean by 'not looking too good'? How bad is it?"

"We don't want to bother you with details," my dad said. "You should be focusing on hockey. And we have a solution, anyway. I've been talking to Brett Gaviston, and he's got it all worked out." Dad stopped to shake his head admiringly. "He's a hell of a businessman, son. A hell of an agent. He understands about the player needing support in all areas of his life, not just on the ice. He's ready to help us out with this."

"How?"

"He's going to give us a loan. Well, give it to you, technically. That's why we have to wait until you turn eighteen. It'll seem like a lot of money, maybe, but that's just because you're used to this nickel-and-dime league. By big league standards, it'll be chump change."

I swallowed hard. "Who repays the loan?" I asked as quietly as I could.

My dad smiled as if I was being silly. "Like I said, Tyler: Once you're in the show, it'll be chump change."

"How much?"

"We don't have the exact numbers worked out," he said way too casually. "We'll have that all sorted out by the time you're ready to sign."

"*Roughly* how much?" I was working hard to stay cool, but it wasn't easy.

"Less than two hundred," he said soothingly.

I stared at him. Two hundred dollars made no sense—I could pay that off now. But the only other option was insane. "Two hundred *grand*? Are you fucking kidding me?"

"Watch your language," he said, looking pointedly at my mother.

I turned to look at her. "Mom, are you fucking kidding me? Two hundred *thousand* dollars?"

"At the most," she said quickly. She reached for my face as if to do her fingertip trick again, but I stepped away. There were tears in her eyes as she said, "They're going to foreclose on the house, baby. And the other loans... We might need to look at bankruptcy. We don't know. There's just...there's just not enough money."

"What if I don't make it to the show?" I asked through gritted teeth. "What if I get drafted but never play? What if I get injured next week and can't come back? You guys want me to be two hundred grand in debt to some asshole—"

"He's *not* an asshole," my dad said angrily. "He's your agent! He looks out for your interests!"

"More like he's *your* agent," I said. "Seems like you're

the one he's looking out for."

"Like I said," he said through tight lips, "*he* understands the importance of family."

"The team's loading up," I said. Thankfully, it was true. "I have to go." I saw Trina and Travis coming across the parking lot and started toward them. I'd say good-bye, then escape.

"We'll talk about this tomorrow," my dad called after me.

I was sure we would. After I'd dragged Travis into another quick hug and given Trina a better one, I climbed onto the bus and slumped down in my usual seat.

Winslow slammed down into the seat next to me and punched my shoulder. "You better get used to this shit, Mr. Grumpy."

"What?" I asked. He expected me to get used to my parents trying to use me as their meal ticket?

"Publicity is part of the job. They love us. You need to get used to it."

Oh. He thought I was just annoyed by the day of community events. I *wished* that was all I had to be pissed off about. "This is the worst one, isn't it?" I tried to remember the other promotional events we had scheduled through the year. Most of the rest of them were with kids, so we'd usually get to actually play a little floor hockey or something, and that made them easier to handle.

"I'm not talking about this bush league shit," Winslow scoffed. "You need to get used to it for when you get drafted. The show is going to make all this look like kiddy time."

Jesus Christ, I could not handle one more person making that assumption, especially not Winslow. He knew better. "Go bug someone else," I said. "I'm not in the mood."

"Is it a superstition?" Christiansen was staring at us from across the aisle. "Not talking about getting drafted. Is it bad luck?"

"*It's a game, and they don't tell us the rules,*" Winslow said. He'd made his voice high and squeaky, nothing like mine, but he was clearly mimicking me all the same. "*Nobody knows what they're looking for. It's impossible to predict. You can't control it so you shouldn't think about it.*"

"So which part of that is wrong?" I asked, staring him down.

"Uh, how about the part where every hockey analyst on the continent is predicting that you go first round?"

"We're *pre-season*, Winslow. They don't know what they're talking about, not yet. Those lists don't mean shit." I looked across at Christiansen. He was so young he probably still believed in Santa Claus, but that didn't mean he should buy Winslow's crap. "You can't plan for it," I said. "You can't…" Jesus, you couldn't take out hundreds of thousands of dollars in loans hoping to pay them back when you made it. But you also couldn't let your family down. You couldn't sit by while your baby brother and sister were kicked out of the only home they'd ever known, couldn't just watch while your parents declared bankruptcy. Not if there was anything you could do to stop it. "Fuck," I groaned. I turned and looked out the window, and after a moment's silence Winslow punched me again, gentler this time.

"Fine. We won't talk about it. Let's talk about Christiansen instead. Did you see him trip over the blue line yesterday in the third period?" He turned to grin at the younger player. "What'd it do, jump out at you?"

"Shut up," the kid said, but he was clearly happy to be

included in the conversation.

I kept staring out the window, half-listening to Winslow as he teased every rookie on the bus. I wished I could just freeze things like they were right then. No draft, no NHL, no agents, and no loans. I wanted to just be a kid, playing hockey and hanging out with his friends. Well, I wanted to be a teenager, old enough to have a hot, smart girlfriend who seemed to like sex just about as much as I did. Yeah, that was important. Hockey, friends, and Karen. That was all I wanted. But I knew I was going to be getting quite a bit more.

Chapter Twenty-Two

Tuesday was the first day of school, but that didn't mean I had to give up on all my summer routine. I woke up before my alarm and practically sprinted out of the house and down to the park. I was eager to get away from all the family drama, and just as enthusiastic about seeing Tyler again. It was scary how much I'd missed him the day before.

I stretched while I sat on the grass waiting for him, and just as my stomach was beginning the process of tightening in anxiety he appeared, jogging easily from the direction of his billet. I stood up and waved to him, he waved back, and then I had nothing to do but stand there like an idiot as he made his way closer.

"Hi," he said, coming to a stop in front of me.

"Hi," I responded. We were pretty smooth.

He was looking at me as if he was trying to read my

expression, and when he took a half-step closer I wiggled my eyebrows a little. I'm not sure exactly what I was trying to convey, but I got the result I was hoping for: he relaxed a little, stepped right into my space, and leaned down to kiss me.

Kissing Tyler made me understand the old cliché about people having chemistry, because there *had* to be something more than simple bodily mechanics going on to make me feel the way I did. It was like my whole body was changing state, going from solid to liquid, heating up and flowing toward him. He had one hand on my jaw, light and gentle, while the other was spread out on the small of my back, strong as it pulled me toward him. I wanted to stay there with him forever, wanted to keep going, strip down and rediscover each other right there on the grass.

But we weren't at our secluded beach anymore, and it was full daylight. He resisted a little when I started to pull away, but then his hand released me and caught me when I staggered from the letdown. "Not the time or place," I gasped.

"We should blow off school," he suggested. "Nothing ever happens on the first day anyway. We could spend the whole day…" He didn't finish the sentence, just gave me an eyebrow wiggle of his own.

"And how would the Rangers feel about that?"

"Raiders," he corrected with a grin. Then his expression grew more serious. "They wouldn't be impressed," he admitted. He shook his head as if there was more to it than he was telling me, then nodded. "Yeah. You're right. I have to go to school. And I want to run. So you, missy, you had just better keep that luscious body away from me. I am a man, and I can't be expected to control myself; as a woman, it's your duty to—"

He didn't seem completely surprised by the raspberry I blew in his direction. He was right about the rest of it, though. We needed to go to school, we wanted to run, so we should get to it.

It wasn't easy. We started off in the woods together, and where the path narrowed he took the lead. That meant I got a beautiful view of his body working the way it was meant to, and I can't say my dirty mind didn't remind me of a few other ways that his body could function. When we looped out into the grassy area, I sped up to run beside him, and when we got back to the narrow part of the path I sprinted ahead. Let *him* be the tortured one this time around.

Even with our good intentions, we quit earlier than we usually did. We stretched out on the grass a little and then Tyler said, "It's important to cool down properly. Maybe we should take another lap of the woods, just walking."

"If I go into those woods with you I am *not* going to be 'cooling down,'" I retorted.

He grinned, looked at his watch, and looked back at me with a mischievous expression. "That'd be so bad?"

God, I was crazy about him. Not just the physical, although that was certainly taking a big role in my feelings right then. But I'd thought he was hot long before I got to know him, and I hadn't been this out of control. No, the crazy was coming from my brain, or my heart or whatever, not from my body. I wanted to make him smile, and I wanted to tell him my secrets and hear all of his. Sure, maybe I wanted to do a lot of that stuff with no clothes on, but even *with* clothes on it seemed like a better way to spend the day than going to some stupid school.

I thought of Natalie and how much she already had on her plate, and I made a face and scooted a little farther away from him. "I need to be good," I said.

"For how long? I've got practice 'til about six, then I have to eat...probably 'til six thirty? Then curfew at ten. No-body's going to give us homework on the first day of classes, so that's three and a half hours. Got any plans?"

"Hmmm...I was thinking about washing my hair."

He tugged gently on my ponytail. "Seems clean to me."

"Well, then, I guess I'm free. You want to go to the lake?"

"Yeah," he said. "Sounds good." Now that we had a plan, it seemed easier for us to stand up and move away from each other, at least a little.

It still took us a while to make the final break, and by the time I got home everyone else was already up and eating breakfast. Will frowned at me. "You need to hurry up; you don't want to be late on the first day. Matt's driving—he'll be leaving in half an hour."

Which gave me plenty of time, considering my traditional easy-care makeup and hair routine, but I didn't want to argue with him about that. "Actually, Tyler said he'd come by and pick me up." I felt guilty saying it in front of Miranda, but I didn't think she was so weak that she needed me to be sneaking around just to spare her feelings.

And she actually managed a tight smile in my direction. "Good. If people are talking about that, it'll give them less energy to talk about anything else."

"Happy to serve," I said, and I poured myself a bowl of cereal. Matt handed me the milk jug, and Will stayed cautiously silent, obviously not wanting to disturb the détente.

I tweaked Sara's jaunty ponytail. "First day of high school—you excited?"

She shrugged then reached over and pulled on *my* ponytail. "First day at a new school—*you* excited?"

Yeah, we were just as sickening as I'd thought the family was when I first arrived, but it felt a bit different when you were one of the people rolling around in the sugar pile.

School turned out to be a bit better than I'd expected, too. I admit, I was a bit nervous, but my sweaty palms were a little cooler because one of them was pressed against Tyler's. We ended up having English together, and Cooper was in my biology class, so it was only calculus where I didn't know anybody. I was hoping to drop that course, anyway, so I didn't worry about it too much. Lunch was spent with the hockey player crowd, Tyler hovering around protectively until Dawn shooed him off to get us some fries and tucked her bright red head in next to mine.

"You're doing okay, right? Having fun? Everything's good?"

"Way better than I expected."

She smiled at me, then said, "You make Tyler happy."

It was nice to hear, but a bit weird, too. "Is he usually unhappy?"

"He's usually kind of tense. He's a worrier, always looking for the worst case scenario. I think you make him a bit more optimistic."

"I think he does the same for me."

"Nice," she said. "Me and Cooper don't work that way. He's super-responsible, I'm a bit of a flake; so we balance each other out, which is good, but we end up fighting all the time, which isn't great."

It was maybe a bit more than I needed to hear about this girl I'd only known for a couple days, but it felt good to have a friend. "Tyler and I haven't actually had a fight yet." I frowned. "But I guess we haven't known each other all that long. It *feels* like a long time, but it really hasn't been."

"Sometimes things just click," she said wisely. I have no idea what TV show or movie she was pulling her wisdom out of, but I liked it.

And as the week wore on, I began to think maybe she was right. It seemed like part of my life *had* clicked. School was good, especially when I got into history instead of calculus. Tyler was good, and we drove out to the lake almost every night. Even home was good, as long as I could overlook the fact that the other kids were miserable. I mean, we weren't fighting all the time, and nobody was looking over my shoulder or bugging me to share my feelings. The talk of therapists had been abandoned, as far as I could tell, and Will may have noticed that I was gone for a few hours a night but he certainly didn't ask me where I was going or what I was doing.

Yeah, the whole thing should have been pretty sweet. Except I *couldn't* overlook the other kids' misery, and I couldn't help missing Natalie. Her kids called her all the time to check in, but it seemed weird for me to do that, so I was cut off entirely. It shouldn't have mattered, but it did. She wasn't *my* mom, but she was *a* mom, and that was the best I had. Except with her gone, I didn't even have that. I played my mom's phone message to myself, but it didn't really help. I wanted to talk to someone, not hear words that no longer had any meaning, no matter how beloved the voice was.

So when I came home after running on Sunday morning

and saw Natalie's car in the driveway, I was totally excited. Tyler was out of town, playing an exhibition game in Brampton that afternoon, and I'd been facing a day of moping around and pretending that I was still an independent person who could have fun without her boyfriend. But if Natalie was back, my schedule was looking up.

I tried to seem natural as I pushed the back door open. When I saw the scene in the kitchen, my enthusiasm dropped dramatically. All the kids were there, and Will and Natalie, and they looked over at me as if they'd forgotten I even lived there and couldn't figure out what I was doing in their home. Natalie was the first to recover.

"Karen," she said, and she smiled tiredly at me. "I'm glad you're back. Will and I were just talking to the kids."

"Yeah, they're telling us how much they love us, and how they love each other, too." Miranda's voice was razor-sharp, and I was glad she wasn't slashing in my direction. "It's been super."

"We do love you all, and we *do* love each other," Natalie said firmly. Then she looked at Will, clearly giving him another of her wordless commands.

He looked like he'd rather be removing his own appendix, but he finally said, "We love each other, but we need some time apart. In order to work on our relationship and figure out the best way to go forward." They were clearly words supplied by Natalie, but he seemed like he was at least trying to mean them. He sounded a bit more natural when he said, "Nothing's decided, nothing's final, we just... We need some time. It didn't make sense for her to be away, not when I know how important she is to you guys, and how she runs this house so well." He looked at her, clearly hoping for a reprieve, but her face stayed stony. He winced, then said, "So I'm going to be moving out for a while. Not forever! Just for a bit. I'll still be here all the time, and I'll still see you; I'll just be sleeping somewhere else."

"Sleeping *with* someone else?" Miranda sneered. I'd been on the receiving end of her anger often enough that I was tempted to feel bad for Will, but then I remembered how much he deserved it.

But apparently Natalie disagreed. "We're not doing that," she said, her voice just as firm as when she'd set down the boundaries between me and Miranda. "The challenges your father and I are facing are between the two of us. We both still love all of you, and we both plan to treat you all with respect and be treated the same way in return." She turned to her daughter and said, "I don't need you to fight my battles for me. I don't *want* you to fight my battles. Is that understood?"

"It's not just *your* battle," Miranda protested. "This affects everyone in the family! It was bad enough when…" She glanced in my direction, remembered that we'd been doing pretty well with our crisis-inspired truce, and shrugged her way into a slightly different word choice. "When everyone *thought* they knew what he was up to. But at least there was always a chance that they were wrong. Now, with this happening…they *know*, Mom. And it affects all of us."

"No," Natalie said quietly. "It doesn't. If people know something about Will's behavior, that affects their opinions of *Will*. Anyone who tries to judge any of you based on his actions isn't someone whose opinion you should value."

I wondered if that was a rule that anyone had ever been able to follow, anywhere, and I could tell that Miranda was having about the same reaction. But she stayed quiet, at least.

There wasn't much more to say after that. I snuck away downstairs while the family continued its disintegration above me, and I tried not to think about how much of it was my fault. Sure, Will had been a cheater forever, but Natalie hadn't been faced with a daily, cranky reminder of it until I arrived. *Something* had clearly triggered this change, and finding out that her son was a cheater as well had probably only been part of it.

All the excitement I'd felt when I'd seen Natalie's car was gone. I headed for the shower and tried not to think, but it was hard to avoid it. These weren't my parents. It wasn't my family, not in any real way. So I didn't have any right to feel the loss, but I did anyway. I felt it a lot.

Chapter Twenty-Three

- *TYLER* -

Brett Gaviston, my agent, was at our practice the afternoon of our home opener, sitting up in the stands with my dad. I didn't even want to look in their direction. My dad hadn't said too much more about the loan since he'd first mentioned it; he just sort of talked like it was a done deal, like it had all been decided and we just needed to wait for my birthday to finalize everything.

I'd let myself go along with that. I guess it was what I always did. I argued, I complained, and then I went along with his plans because I didn't want to make a fuss. Even though I knew it was bullshit, a part of me still wanted to be the good son, the chip off the old block. The star of the family.

I wanted to be the good player, too. I wanted to listen to the coach and make him happy and say that I was just like some other player, some hero that everyone admired.

No matter how much I protested, how much I worried that I wouldn't be able to manage it, I wanted to be the star of the team, too.

Karen didn't really understand it. I'd told her about the loan, and she'd shaken her head and said there was no way she'd ever go along with something like that. I believed her. Karen had no problem standing up to people. She'd say 'no' before the question was even asked. She made me feel weak, sometimes, but then she'd kiss me and I'd forget about all of it.

She was coming to the game that night, but she'd only come to practice once. She'd tried to be a good sport about it, but I'd known she was a bit confused by all the adults in the stands acting as if it really mattered what the kids on the ice were doing, and a bit freaked out by the girls hanging around, waiting to catch the players' attention. I'd tried to explain that there just wasn't much else for people to do in a small town, but she'd pulled out her phone and opened her browser and tried to introduce me to a "little thing called the internet."

"Look alive, Tyler!" my dad yelled from the stands. He was always a bit more vocal when my agent was around. But we were just supposed to be doing a light skate, working out our nerves before the game, so I was doing exactly what I was supposed to be doing. Well, maybe I should have been thinking more about strategies or skills or something else a bit more related to hockey, but my dad couldn't tell what was going on in my brain. Thankfully.

When I got off the ice, he and Gaviston were waiting for me. "Get changed and we'll go get something to eat," my dad said.

"Something light," Gaviston added. "You can have a big meal after the game tonight."

"I need to be back at the arena by four thirty," I said. Really our pre-game meeting was scheduled for five thirty, but I generally liked some time alone before games, and I absolutely wanted as little time with my dad and Gaviston as possible.

"No problem." My dad sounded impatient. I guess it was okay for me to take my mind off the game as long as I was sending my thoughts in the direction he wanted.

So I got changed, and we went to one of the big chain restaurants up on the hill, and even though I was tempted to order half their menu, just to piss Gaviston off, I settled for a chicken breast and Greek salad.

He ordered a burger with a side of fries, the bastard. And he and my dad had beer while I got a Coke. It was a good way to remind me that I was just a kid, I guess. I mean, I wouldn't have been drinking before a game no matter who I was with, and it wasn't like I had trouble buying beer whenever I wanted. So the drinks didn't mean anything, really, except that somehow they did.

Then Gaviston started talking about the loan. "It'll be a flexible repayment schedule," he said reassuringly. "If it takes you a few years to find your place in the league, you don't need to worry about paying it off right away. I'll charge interest at a rate set by one of the major banks, so that'll be fair. You'll repay me as you can. The only limitation is that you won't be able to sign with any other agent until the loan is paid in full. But that's not a serious limit, is it?" His smile was confident, as if he couldn't imagine me ever wanting to work with anyone but him.

But if there was no way I'd ever want a different agent, then there was no reason for him to put that clause in the loan contract. You don't need to force someone to do something they'd want to do anyway.

I didn't say anything, just sipped my Coke and waited for it all to be over. I knew what Karen would say: she'd say it wouldn't be over until I *made* it be over. But I didn't know how to do that, not without hurting people I cared about.

It usually makes me uncomfortable when people recognize me and approach me in public, but this time when I saw a kid at a nearby table sneaking looks at me and then whispering to his dad, I gave him a big grin and pulled my shirt around so he could see the *Raiders* logo. He beamed at me, and his dad gave me a questioning look. I nodded and the kid shot out of his chair like it was an ejector seat.

"Tyler MacDonald! Tyler MacDonald! We're going to the game tonight, me and my dad and my friend and his dad. We're going to see you play. It's going to be a great game, right? I bet you get ten goals. And twenty assists! We're going to be sitting behind the bench. Maybe you'll see us there. If you do, you could wave, okay? But you don't have to. Not if you're busy with the game. But I'll see you, right up close."

"Closer than you are now?"

The kid looked puzzled, then shook his head. "No. But now you're just…you're just normal. Tonight you'll be special."

I knew what he meant: the skates and the uniform and the attention everyone gave me. I *did* seem more special at the rink. But underneath it all, it was still just me. Just somebody normal. "I'll look for you," I said. "Do you play?"

"Defense," he said proudly. "But I score goals, too, when I can."

"Nice. An all-rounder. I try to play defense when I can, so we'd be good on the same line, right? You could take the opportunities for scoring when they come, and you'd know that I'd drop back and help cover the defense."

His eyes were wide. Kids loved it when you talked about playing on the same line as them. But then he shook his head. "If I was on the same line as you, I think you should be the one taking the shots," he said seriously.

I shrugged. "Maybe. You'll have to do a few years of growing before we'd be in the same league; maybe by then your shot will be better than mine."

His eyes had gone back to being wide. "We could be in the NHL together?"

Or the same bar league. But I probably didn't need to spew all that insecurity over an innocent kid so I shrugged and said, "Who knows? Maybe."

His dad came over then, we shook hands, and they wished me luck, then went back to their own table. Gaviston gave me an approving nod. "Being good with fans is important. It's an intangible, not right there on the scouting report, but teams notice."

"Not everything's about getting drafted."

Gaviston and my dad both looked at me like I was speaking Martian. Gaviston was the one who leaned in and hissed, "You need to change that attitude, son. This isn't… It's not high school. You can't goof off and make up the credits next year. You can't take a gap year and go hiking across Europe and come back and expect university to be just waiting for you. You do *not* have that flexibility." He shook his head as if shocked that he had to explain this to me. "*This season* is your chance. Every game, every *shift*, they all count. If you screw this up, there're no do-overs." He leaned back and actually picked up his knife and pointed it at me. It was a dull table knife, and he was across the table so it wasn't actually a threat, but it was pretty intense all the same. "So, no, Tyler. You're wrong. This year? *Every* goddamn thing *is* about getting drafted. You want to go out to eat? Fine, as long as you're making contacts while you're out there, doing things that make scouts hear that you're a fan favorite so teams will want to draft you. You want a summer job? Okay, because it'll give you some spending money for the year so you can focus on hockey and do well so teams will want to draft you. You want a girlfriend? Fine. Because she'll help you relax so you can play better so *teams will want to draft you*. Are you getting my point here, Tyler?"

It wasn't exactly subtle. "I hear you," I said. Then I looked at my watch. There was still lots of time, even for my extra-early deadline, but I was ready to get out of there. "I should get back to the rink. Get my head in the game so I can play well and teams will want to draft me. Right?"

Gaviston laughed and beamed at me like I was a hero. I wasn't sure if he'd actually missed the sarcasm or was just choosing to ignore it. Either way, he waved the server over and got our bill, so I wasn't going to complain. We walked back out to his rental, and I folded myself into the back seat and stared out the window while the grownups had their important conversations up front.

When we got to the rink, they parked and for a bit I was afraid they were going to come inside with me and keep up the harassment right until game time, but instead Gaviston clapped me on the shoulder and said, "Stay focused, Tyler. This is your season. This is your chance."

"Don't screw it up," my dad said darkly.

Those were the words that echoed in my head as I made my way into the deserted change room. *Don't screw it up. Don't screw it up.* I slumped down onto the bench in front of my locker and stared at the ceiling. *Don't screw it up.* It seemed so simple, when it was just words. But when I had to translate the words into actions, everything got a bit more complicated.

Chapter Twenty-Four

- KAREN -

I don't think they knew I was home. Looking back, that's what makes sense. I was supposed to be down at the beach with Miranda and Sara, but I'd come home early because I was strangely nervous about Tyler's game that night. It wasn't his playing that had me concerned; I knew he'd do well and didn't care if he didn't, except for the part where he'd be upset about it. I was more worried about it being one more public statement of our coupledom. Dawn had told me that the local reporters had wanted to interview her the year before when Cooper was made alternate captain, and I didn't want to be that close to the spotlight. And even if the press didn't care, I was supposed to be sitting in the players' complimentary ticket area, which Dawn said meant a little extra attention. Will and the kids were going to be at the game so maybe I should have sat with them, but Tyler had offered the ticket and I'd agreed, so I couldn't back out.

Anyway, I was nervous and I went home early to shower and get dressed. Dawn had come over the day before and helped sort through my wardrobe, trying to find something that would look natural for a hockey game without sacrificing my personal style. She didn't dress conventionally, either, although her look was more rocker than retro, but at least she understood that I wasn't trying to look like a kid in a magazine. I was happy with the vintage dress and jean jacket combo we'd come up with, but it wasn't really enough to keep me calm.

There'd been no one home when I arrived, but as I came up the stairs I heard voices in the kitchen. The grandperfects, and they didn't sound pleased. I was hoping to sneak out the back door, but I paused at the top of the stairs to plan my escape.

I glanced into the kitchen and saw Natalie standing at the sink staring out the window as if she wished she could climb through it. I hesitated, wondering if I should go in to give her a little support.

"If you're going to do it, you need to *do* it," her mother was saying. "I've got the name of Cynthia Pearson's lawyer. You *know* what a good job he did. You should get the accounts frozen, start keeping track of every penny you spend on the kids, or on the house or the cars. If you're doing this, you can't mess around."

"And you need to get that girl out of here," her father said. "Why the hell are you babysitting his bastard? If it came down to it in court, could that be used as evidence that you *approve* of his infidelities? It's sure going to make it hard for you to argue that you didn't *know* about them."

"Legalities aside," her mother said, "the whole point of bringing the girl up here was to make *him* take responsibility for his mistakes. Instead, here you are again, covering for him, letting him get away with—"

I didn't want to hear any more. I wanted to sneak out and pretend I hadn't heard it at all, but I guess my purse banged on the door, just a little but at exactly the wrong time. Natalie turned and saw me. Her face was drawn tight, and she looked about ten years older than she was. "Karen—" she started, but I didn't think I wanted to hear any more.

"I'm off to the game," I said brightly, my smile forced but wide. "I'm going to get dinner there, I think." Because there was no way on Earth I was going to sit down for a meal with the grandperfects. "Gotta go." And I was off, trotting down the steps and around the corner of the house, then sprinting for a few glorious strides as soon as I was sure I was out of their sight. I slowed again when I got to the sidewalk but kept moving fast.

Nobody came after me. I might have heard Natalie call my name, but I'm not even sure about that. Probably I imagined it. Why would she chase me? What was there to say? Her parents were right. I had no right to a place in that house, and if Will was gone for good, I guessed I was, too. It made sense, and it was crazy that I hadn't already thought of it. Yeah, I couldn't expect Natalie to keep babysitting Will's bastard. I just had no idea where I was supposed to go.

So I headed for the arena. I was a couple hours early, but maybe Tyler would be there, and maybe he'd have a couple minutes for me. Maybe that would be enough. Just a kiss, a few moments with his warm body making mine feel alive.

I was in the parking lot, heading for the front door, when

I heard an unfamiliar voice call my name. I turned to see a man in a business suit jogging across the parking lot toward me. "Karen," he repeated. "Right?" He saw my hesitation and smiled as he offered his hand. "I'm Brett Gaviston, Tyler's agent."

"Oh." I said, shaking his hand a bit tentatively. I knew Tyler had mixed feelings about his agent, but it seemed best to be polite. "It's nice to meet you, Mr. Gaviston."

"Nice to meet you, too. And, please, call me Brett."

I nodded to show that I understood, then waited. Were we supposed to be making small talk?

Brett checked his watch, then looked at me. "You're here early."

I shrugged. "I guess so."

"That's great. It gives us some time to talk. Why don't we sit over here?" He had his hand on my elbow, not really grabbing hold, just sort of guiding me. I could have gotten free if I'd tried, but it would have felt rude. So I let myself be taken over to the stone bench beneath the trees. He sat down and looked up at me expectantly, so I sat down, too. I wasn't quite sure when I'd gotten so suggestible; I guess I was still kind of numb from everything at the house.

We just sat quietly for a bit, and then Brett said, "This is a big year for Tyler."

I nodded. "The draft, right?"

"That's the goal. Absolutely. But, I'm not sure…" He trailed off, then looked at me apologetically. "You don't want to hear all this."

"All what?"

"All my concerns. My worrying about the future. Tyler's future. That's not something a pretty girl should have to worry about on a beautiful day like today."

Reverse psychology? It seemed so transparent, but, damn, it was still working. "If there's something you think I should know, I'm happy to listen."

"Are you? Of course you are. Because you care about Tyler." He nodded. "That's nice. It truly is. I mean, a lot of people—a lot of young women—care about him. But you're special, right? Because *he* cares about *you*."

I didn't feel too special right then, but I shrugged. "This is what you wanted to tell me?"

Another smile. "I'm not sure I need to tell you anything, really. I mean, you're a smart girl. A compassionate girl. And you care about Tyler. You know how much he's given up to get to where he is. How he barely sees his mother, or his brother and sister. He was granted exceptional player status to enter the OHL. Did you know that? So he came down a year early, when he was only fifteen. Left his family behind, started a whole new life in a new town. But you know how hard that is, of course."

He leaned back and looked up into the leaves over our heads for a moment, like he was lost in reverie. I was getting pretty tired of the performance, but I wanted to see where he was taking it. So I waited patiently, and finally he said, "You haven't seen how hard he works during the season, of course. Not yet. You haven't seen him playing hurt, haven't seen how much it bothers him when he makes a mistake in a game, or how much he hates to lose. Hates letting the team down."

"He loves the game." I sounded kind of defensive, even to my own ears.

"He does," Brett agreed. "And he's got a chance to make

all the pain pay off. All the sacrifices. But he must have told you that it's far from a sure thing?"

Tyler had definitely told me that. Winslow and the other players I'd met seemed a lot more confident, but Tyler said he wasn't really big enough for the NHL, and probably wasn't fast enough, either. "I thought maybe he was just being hard on himself."

"Realistic, more like it." Brett shook his head. "If Tyler's going to be drafted—if he's going to get the chance to make his dream come true and get the payoff for everything he's given up—he needs to play better this year than he's ever played before. He needs *everything* to go right." He smiled at me again, this time with a little sadness mixed into his expression. "He needs to be totally focused on hockey. No distractions whatsoever."

Oh. He was talking about me. I wasn't sure how to respond, so I just stared at him, and after a few moments he shrugged. "I'm not saying you shouldn't have fun together. It's just…he's a good guy. A caring guy. He wants to help people. And you?" Another shrug. "You seem like you could use quite a bit of help."

"What? You don't know anything about me."

"Of course I do. You've been here long enough to know how small towns work. I know plenty about you, and I know how things are going at your house." The smile was gone, now. "I know that things have gone downhill there since you arrived. And maybe they'll be able to pull themselves back together—I don't know. But you need to understand that a family is a lot more resilient than a fledgling hockey career. If your dad has a few rough months, that's too bad for him, but he can bounce back. If *Tyler* has a rough few months? Now, with every scout on the continent watching every breath he takes? That'd be it for him. For all of his dreams. He could be someone who makes millions of dollars playing a game he loves, or he could be another washed-up minor-leaguer, another unemployed drywaller trying to live his dreams through his son." He waited again, and when he saw I had nothing to say, he gentled his voice. "That's how important the next few months are to Tyler. Do you understand what I'm saying?"

I nodded. I understood. I wasn't sure how I felt about any of it, but I understood it.

"Good. So you need to make a choice. If you can be the right kind of girlfriend for Tyler? If you can be supportive, someone he comes to for fun and relaxation, someone who knows her place and her role? Then you can help him out. But if you want to drag him into your mess? If you want to make your relationship all about *you* and what you need? You'll be hurting him. You could be *ruining* him."

"I'm not going to hurt him."

He stared at me, then nodded slowly. "I believe you. I believe that you wouldn't hurt him on purpose. But, honestly—can you stop him from hurting himself? Because if he knows you're upset about something, he's going to want to help you, isn't he? That's the kind of person he is. But he can't *be* that kind of person. Not this year."

I didn't want to hear any of this. I just wanted to find Tyler, and…distract him? Make him worry about me instead of about the game? Wasn't that why I'd been coming to the arena in the first place?

"I think you can see the problem," Brett said gently. "Even talking to him about this conversation? Asking him what he thinks you should do? Even doing that will be a distraction. He'll be worrying about this instead of about his game. Do you see that?"

"It should be his choice," I managed to say.

Brett frowned. "He's made his choice, Karen. Every morning when he got out of bed before dawn to go to the rink, he made his choice. When he left his family behind so he could play hockey, he made his choice. He's made it so many times already. But now? If he feels guilty, if he feels like he has to protect you and look after you? Is that really a choice *he's* making, or is it a choice *you're* making?"

I felt a bit sick. I'd done nothing but create trouble since I got to town. First the Beacons, and now Tyler. "What am I supposed to do?" I whispered.

Brett put a kindly hand on my shoulder. I wanted to shrug it off, but I couldn't seem to find the energy. "A clean break is probably best," he said gently. "After the game tonight, you can just tell him you need some space. Tell him you want to be friends, or whatever, but that there are too many changes in your life and you need to keep things stable. That would work, right?"

Of course it would work. It was almost the truth. It was what I'd already told Tyler, and he'd believed me then and given me the space I thought I needed. And I'd gone running to him as soon as I'd been upset, dragging him away from his team dinner, acting like I was the only one who mattered.

"I don't know," I said.

"I think you do." He smiled again, and I really wanted to punch him right in his smarmy face. He was a con man, trying to control Tyler because if Tyler made lots of money, Brett would make lots of money. I wasn't stupid enough to miss all that. But I also wasn't stupid enough to ignore the truth of what he was saying.

"I need to go," I said, pushing myself off the bench.

"Be back for the game," Brett said firmly. "Until you've officially broken up, you need to be supportive."

I didn't answer. I just walked away, even though I had no idea where I was going to go.

Chapter Twenty-Five

- TYLER -

I pulled the truck into the lot at the park and wasn't too surprised to see someone Karen-shaped sitting on one of our benches. Her step-mother had called me at the rink, looking for Karen, and said just enough to freak me out. I'd tried Karen's cell, and when she hadn't answered I'd convinced Coach to let me take a quick road trip. He'd made it clear I wouldn't start in the game if I didn't get back in time for the pre-game skate, but that was okay. It was still early in the season, and our rookies needed ice time. Coach wouldn't have let me go if he'd thought it was a big deal.

But now that I'd found Karen, I wasn't quite sure what I was supposed to do about it. Mrs. Beacon had been a bit vague on the phone, just saying that Karen had overheard something she shouldn't, and they needed to talk, and I should tell Karen that nothing she'd heard meant anything.

Probably something with Miranda, I figured, so I hadn't asked too many more questions.

Sitting there in the parking lot, though, I wished I had a better idea what I was getting into. I reminded myself that this was Karen and I needed to just get over myself and go make sure she was okay, and that helped. So I headed across the grass toward her, and when she saw me coming, she straightened up like she was bracing herself. Like something unpleasant was coming. It totally threw me off.

"You okay?" I asked, trying to sound casual and gentle.

"What are you doing here? You've got a game." She sounded like she was accusing me of something. Sounded kind of like my father, to be honest.

But I tried to ignore that. "Mrs. Beacon called. She said she was worried about you, and said you weren't answering your phone. And you didn't answer when I called, either, so that made me a bit worried myself. So…here I am."

"Your game," she said. "You need to be at the game. You can't be chasing me around, dealing with my stupid shit, not when you've got something important going on."

"Okay, well, it's not a big deal. It's just hockey, right? Just the Corrigan Falls Rangers? Nothing to get upset about. But, yeah, I should get back as soon as I can. So, do you want to tell me what's going on? Or maybe just call Mrs. Beacon and talk to her?"

She stared at me, then looked away, over to the forest, her face kind of twisted around, and I realized that she was trying not to cry. It shouldn't have felt weird to sit down beside her, but it did, especially when I felt her body tense up. "What can I do? I'll help, but you've got to tell me what you need. Seriously, I have no idea what's going on."

"No, you don't," she said, and she sounded angry. "You have no idea, and it's none of your business. Look, I have my own stuff, okay? It's *mine*, and I'll deal with it. I don't need your help."

That was pretty clear. It felt wrong to pretend there was nothing going on, but it also felt wrong to ignore her instructions. "So you want me to just leave? Can you at least call home and check in with her?"

Karen whirled toward me. She wasn't trying to control her tears anymore. "You need to go to your game. Do you not understand that? This is a big year for you, and you can't…you can't…" She stopped talking, then, and turned right around so only her back was facing me.

"I'm fine," I tried, but she shook her head really hard, making it clear she wasn't listening to me. "What the hell?" I said, mostly to myself. Everything had been fine, and something had happened, and now everything was wrong. And Karen was suddenly obsessed with me playing hockey? "Should I call your step-mom?"

She shook her head then sat up straight. I could see her taking a deep breath, and then letting it out and taking another. Trying to calm herself down. I was definitely in favor of that idea. Except that after another breath, she turned to face me, and something in her expression made my stomach clench.

"This isn't working for me," she said. She wouldn't meet my eyes. "I need more space."

"What? Because of…what? Because you heard someone say something mean about you? Is that what happened? Jesus, Karen, who the hell cares what someone else says, and what does that have to do with you and me?" I needed to figure this out. "Did you hear someone say something about *me?* I honestly don't think I have any secrets, but if you heard something you don't like, you should tell me what it is. You need to give me the chance to at least explain it, okay?"

"It's not about you," she practically snarled. "It's about me. And I don't have to explain it to you, or give you a chance to explain it to me, or anything else. It's not your choice, it's *mine*."

"But—"

"Leave me alone, Tyler. It's over. Go play your stupid game."

It didn't make any sense. But maybe these things never did. Maybe I was just one more in a long line of idiots who thought things were going well when they really weren't. I mean, Karen wasn't the first girl I'd slept with, but she was my first real girlfriend. And this was my first real dumping. Maybe they always felt this way. Maybe one person was always mad, and the other one was always shocked, almost dizzy with confusion and fear and denial. "I could call you later," I tried.

She stood up and took a few steps away from the benches. "I won't answer."

I had no idea what to do. I don't remember deciding to go back to the truck, but somehow, I was in it, staring through the windshield at Karen, back on the bench, with her knees all curled up like she was hugging herself. Hugging herself because she had no one else to do it. I found my phone and dialed, and when Mrs. Beacon answered I said, "Karen's at the park, the one down from your house, with the forest. She's…upset, I guess. She didn't want to talk to me." Didn't want to talk to me ever again, but I wasn't going to tell that to someone I barely knew. "But maybe you should go see her and make sure she's okay."

"I'm on my way," Mrs. Beacon said, and she hung up.

I sat there in my truck until I saw Mrs. Beacon pull in a few spots down, and then I backed out and headed for the arena. Karen didn't want me. I might as well go play my stupid game.

Chapter Twenty-Six

- KAREN -

At first when the shadow fell on me, I thought it was Tyler, and I knew I wouldn't be strong enough to send him away again. I'd barely been able to do it the first time. I was too selfish to do what was best for him, even if I knew I'd end up hating myself for ruining his chances.

So when I half-turned and saw Natalie standing there, I was torn between relief and disappointment. It took me a moment to realize how upset she looked, and to trace her expression back to any sort of source.

"I'm so sorry you heard that," she said, and I honestly thought she was talking about hearing what Tyler's agent had said to me.

I figured out what she meant before I opened my mouth, but I didn't have to change the words I was going to say. "It's good that I heard it. I needed to hear the truth."

"The truth?" Natalie sounded angry. "The truth is that I'm not a little girl and my parents don't make my decisions for me. The truth is that you're part of this family. Part of *my* family. You have a home with me, a home with your brother and your sisters, for as long as you want it. Do you understand?"

It should have made me happy, but it didn't seem nearly as important as it had a couple hours earlier. "I wrecked your marriage," I said.

"Oh, please." She still sounded kind of impatient. "You don't have that kind of power, Karen. Will and I damaged our marriage. His actions and my inactions. He ignored our vows, and I let him. That's nothing to do with you."

"So it's just a coincidence that it all went wrong a couple weeks after I moved up here? Seriously?"

Natalie sighed. "No, I guess it's not a coincidence. I suppose you were a bit of a catalyst. And Matt's behavior was a bit of a catalyst. Honestly, hearing about Miranda and Tyler, realizing that my daughter was becoming a woman and was looking at *me* as an example of how to deal with relationships and how to demand the respect we deserve? Another catalyst. Sending my babies off for their last year of high school, starting to look seriously at where they'll be this time next year? That's another doozy." She pulled her legs up onto the bench and sat cross-legged, facing me. "Life is complicated. Relationships are complicated. But there are some things that are simple, and one of those things is your place in this family. I know it's not traditional, and I'm sure we'll still have plenty of adjustments, but you absolutely belong with us. And I made that crystal clear to my parents."

I tried to say something, tried to at least nod in a coherent way, but instead I just sort of—crumbled. I don't know how else to describe it. If Natalie hadn't been there, I probably would have fallen off the bench, all curled up and sobbing, but she *was* there. She caught me, wrapped her arms around me and let me cry into the hollow between her neck and her shoulder, just like my mom had always done when I'd needed her to.

I don't know how long we stayed like that, but finally I more or less got control of myself and realized that I was probably snotting all over her shirt. But when I pulled away, she smiled gently at me as if she wasn't too concerned about that. "Tyler said you didn't want to talk to him," she said.

"We shouldn't start on that unless you want to get a lot more snot-covered." I tried to laugh, but it came out sounding more like a sob.

"I can always change my shirt." She reached out and took my hand. "What did he do?"

And that set me off again. "Nothing," I managed to say, and then her arms were back around me and I was crying again. This time, though, I tried to keep talking. I didn't want her thinking this was Tyler's fault. I couldn't stand the idea of anyone blaming him for anything—not when he already had way too much to worry about. "It's not him. I just…he needs to focus on the game…this is his draft year. He needs to…needs to…"

Then Natalie's hands were on my shoulders, stronger than I'd expected, and she was holding me away from her so she could look me in the face. "What are you saying, Karen? If he broke up with you to focus on hockey, that's—well, I suppose it's understandable, if that's his priority, but why would you say it's not him?"

"He didn't break up with me." I wanted back at her shoulder, but she held me away, so I kept talking. "I broke up with him. He wouldn't want to hurt me, but that doesn't mean I should be allowed to hurt him. I can't distract him from…from…" I tried to remember all the words that had made such horrible sense when his agent had used them.

"You think you were hurting him, by being with him?" Natalie sounded truly confused. "Oh, baby, why would you think that? Did he say that?"

"Of course not! He wouldn't say something like that." Now it was my turn to want a little distance. "I keep telling you, this wasn't Tyler's idea."

"It was *your* idea?" She sounded kind of skeptical.

"Not…not entirely."

Natalie pulled her sleeves down over her hands and used the fabric to wipe my tears away. Then she took both of my hands in hers. "Okay. We're going to start at the beginning. When you left the house this morning, everything seemed good between you and Tyler. So tell me now — what changed that?"

It felt good to go through it all. I hadn't been able to tell Tyler, but telling Natalie felt almost as good, without worrying that I was guilting her into anything. When I was done, she shook her head at me and said, "Do you really think it's your place to make that kind of decision for Tyler?"

"I care about him. So, I should do what's best for him. Right?"

"How can you know what's best for him without talking to him about it? How would you feel if he made that sort of decision on *your* behalf?"

"I wouldn't like it," I mumbled. I wasn't convinced by

the argument, yet, but there was a tiny flicker of hope growing inside me that maybe I *could* be convinced. Maybe I didn't have to give Tyler up. I gripped her hand more tightly than was probably comfortable. "But don't we have to look out for people we care about? Don't we have to…I don't know, make sacrifices for them? Worry about their happiness instead of our own?"

She leaned back a little, and I could tell she was trying to decide just how much she wanted to say to me. Finally, she smiled and said, "When I first found out about you—about Will and your mother—I thought about leaving him. I had two little babies and not a lot of money, and it would have been hard on my own, but that wasn't why I stayed." Another little smile, this one sad. "I stayed because I loved him. And when he cheated on me again, and again, and again… I stayed. I turned away and pretended I didn't see. I sacrificed my self-respect because I was worried about his happiness. You know what I wish I'd have done?"

"Kicked his ass?"

Her laugh was quick and light, and even though her eyes were wet now, the sound felt real. "Yes. I wish I'd kicked his ass. I wish I'd demanded that he either follow the vows he made to me or have the guts to call off the marriage for good." She shrugged and squeezed my fingers. "I think he'd have stayed. Because he loved me, and he still does. I just never… I never trusted that love. I never let it be tested, never relied on it to pull us through a tough time. Does that make any sense to you?"

"I think so. But Tyler's not cheating on me. If anything, he's cheating on *hockey*, by being with me."

"Do you think hockey cares?"

"Maybe! The way the agent was talking, it could really matter. If Tyler doesn't pay complete attention to everything this year—"

"Or, alternatively, if Tyler doesn't have the release of being able to have fun and be with someone who doesn't care so much about the game?" She tucked a chunk of hair behind my ear. "I can't say what's best for Tyler's hockey career. But I don't think you can, either. I think it's *Tyler's* job to figure that out. I think you need to talk to him about it, and, no. I don't think you need to sacrifice for him and worry about his happiness instead of your own. I think if you're going to be a real team, you need to worry about team happiness. Both of you. Not one more than the other. And I think you need to talk to each other to figure out the best way to make sure you're both happy."

"I can't decide if I believe you because it makes sense, or just because it's what I want to hear."

"Maybe both?" She shrugged nonchalantly. "I mean, I *am* very wise. Very, very wise. So obviously what I say makes sense."

I couldn't believe it, but I actually smiled at her then. "I wish—" I stopped. It might be what I wanted to say, but that didn't mean it was what Natalie would want to hear.

But she peered at me, gently curious. "What?" she prompted.

"I know it wasn't a good situation. I know you got hurt. But it wasn't my mom's fault, really, and I wish you could have met her. I think—I mean, in a different world, one that was less messed up? I think you would have liked each other."

Now it was her turn to be a bit blubbery. Or, okay, maybe

we were both crying a little. "I'm sure I would have, sweetie," Natalie said, and then we leaned together and there was one more hug before she pulled away. "But, now. There's a handsome young man about to step on the ice at the arena, and I think he's probably feeling a bit confused about a few things. Probably a bit upset. Do you want to splash your face off in that fountain over there and I can drive you to the rink? Maybe you can get a word with him before he goes on the ice, or we can make a sign and hold it up in the stands, or we could engage in a madcap scheme to have you apologize over the PA system, or—"

"Let's just try for the 'get a word before he goes on the ice' plan," I said quickly and headed for the fountain. I knew I was behaving like a bit of a maniac, and Tyler would be completely within his rights to not want anything to do with me, but it seemed like the sooner I was able to talk to him, the less chance he'd have to realize he was better off without me.

The cool water made me feel a bit more in control, and I let it run all over my face and my arms before pulling away. I wasn't looking too good, I knew, but Tyler had seen me covered in sweat enough times that I didn't think a little rosiness and a lack of makeup was going to be a big turnoff. "Okay," I said, jogging back to where Natalie was waiting for me. "I'm ready."

"Let's do this," she said, and we headed off toward her minivan like we were on a mission.

Chapter Twenty-Seven

- TYLER -

I drove around for a few extra minutes to make sure I was kind of under control, but I guess it didn't do as much good as I'd thought. As soon as I took one step into the locker room, Coach saw my face and jerked his head at Winslow. I knew what that meant, and sure enough, about two seconds later Chris was looming over me, his face good-natured and totally relaxed.

"I don't need a babysitter," I snapped at him. "I'm the captain. It's my job to look after people, not to be looked after."

Chris nodded and held out his left hand. "I've got a sliver, I think. But it's one of those ones you can't really see, you know? It's right on this finger." He extended his middle finger, flashing me the bird with an innocent smile. "Can you see it?"

"Fuck off, Winslow."

"I thought you were going to look after me. I'm in pain, here." He clutched his chest melodramatically. "'Oh Captain, my Captain'…" He trailed off and shrugged. "And then some other stuff. I don't know what comes next. The point is—I have an invisible sliver, and you're no help at all. That's a nice leadership style you've got there, chief."

Oh, god, if Winslow was calling me 'chief' it meant he planned to keep this up for a lot longer. It was like he thought he could just harass people into being in a good mood, and it was truly frightening how often it actually worked. But in this case, he was out of luck, and any chance he might have had disappeared entirely when I looked over his shoulder and saw my dad making his way into the room.

I pulled my shirt over my head and unbuttoned my jeans. I didn't need Dad bugging me for being late on top of everything else. But I guess losing a piece of clothing wasn't enough to disguise the fact that everyone else in the room was already geared up and I'd barely started, because Dad's first words were, "Where the hell have you been?"

"I had to see somebody," I muttered, pulling my compression shirt over my head.

"Did you see any scouts out there, Mr. MacDonald?" Winslow asked, innocent and bouncy as a damn puppy.

Any other day that would have been enough to distract my dad and I would have owed Winslow huge, but I wasn't so lucky this time. "You had to see that girl," my dad said, ignoring Chris and making 'girl' sound like a dirty word. "God damn it, you should know better. Brett said he had this taken care of."

I froze for a moment, then turned to stare at him.

"What?" I demanded.

I could tell from his reaction that he'd said more than he planned, but of course he couldn't just admit it. "You should know better," he repeated. "This is your big year, and—"

"What did Brett say he'd taken care of?" My voice was low, but there must have been something in it that made my dad take me seriously.

Still, he didn't give up entirely. "He takes care of *everything*. He's your agent and your best friend. He looks out for you, in all ways."

"I'm going to ask once more, and then I'm going to go figure it out myself. What did Brett take care of *with Karen*?"

"Don't use that tone with me," he tried.

I pulled my phone out of my back pocket and headed for the door, punching numbers as I went. When I saw a text from Karen—saw that it had been sent just a couple minutes earlier—I started moving faster.

If you have time, can I talk to you? I messed up. I'm really sorry. I don't think I meant it.

I typed back *Where r u?* as I left the change room and headed toward the back parking lot. I felt a hand on my shoulder and whirled, ready to yell at my dad, and saw Winslow instead. "I can't worry about the game just this second, Winslow!"

He shrugged. "That's cool. But you should do up your pants, chief."

"Shit." I handed him my phone as I worked on my fly, and he peered at the screen with interest.

"She'll meet you in the front lobby," he told me calmly and didn't complain when I grabbed the phone back to see the message for myself.

That meant going back the way we'd come, and of course my dad and now Brett were there, and they tried to intercept me. I brushed past them. There were things I needed to sort out with them, stuff I should have made clear earlier, but it wasn't what I was most worried about right then. So I charged on, dimly aware of Winslow looming behind me, blocking Brett and my dad as well as he could without actually body checking either of them.

Once I got to the lobby, it took a while to find Karen because the area was crowded with people coming in for the game. "Over there," Winslow said and pointed. He was easily three inches taller than me, so he'd seen her first, but as soon as I started moving, the crowd parted a little and there she was. Karen.

She looked unsure, and her face was kind of blotchy, but she was there. She'd texted me, and she'd said she didn't think she meant it, and that made her look more beautiful than she ever had before. I got to her and froze. She'd said she *thought* she didn't mean it. But that wasn't quite enough, was it?

"I'm sorry," she said quickly. "I should have talked to you about it. I thought I was doing the right thing, but I don't think I was. Can we erase everything in the park, and just start over again after the game? I can tell you what happened, and you can tell me what you think we should do."

I had my mouth open to agree, but then my dad was there, stepping between us. He turned to face me, ignoring Karen completely. "Get your ass back in that locker room," he bellowed, and the excited buzz of the crowd faded to nothing as everyone waited to hear what was going to happen next.

Again, I was just about to speak, and again, someone else did it before I could. This time it was Mrs. Beacon, sliding forward with a gentle smile, her hand reaching politely for my dad's forearm. "I think this is something the kids need to work out on their own," she said calmly. "I'm sure Tyler will go back to the game in just a—"

My dad ripped his arm away from Mrs. Beacon so hard she stumbled a little, and then he took an aggressive step toward her. "Stay out of my son's business. We wouldn't be in this mess if you could have kept your husband at home, you dried up bitch!"

I would have done something, once I recovered from the shock, but again I didn't have time, because suddenly Mr. Beacon was there, pushing my dad away from his wife, then hauling off and landing a solid punch right in my dad's face. "Don't talk to my wife like that," he growled.

My dad caught his balance and surged forward, blood streaming from his chin, but I was finally alert enough to step in and catch him. I was dimly aware of Winslow behind me, holding back Mr. Beacon, but mostly I was focused on my dad.

"Calm down and walk away," I told him, still grappling a little, my voice quiet because my mouth was near his ear. "If you walk away now, you and me still have a chance. We might still be able to pull something out of this." I pushed him back then because I wanted to see his face and be sure he understood what I was saying. "The loan, saving the house, everything that *might* work for you? If you walk away now, we can still talk about that. But if you stay here, and you make things worse? That's it. We're done. You understand me?"

His disbelieving stare made it clear that he comprehended

the words, but maybe not the sentiment behind them. "Because of a *girl*?" he whispered.

"No." I glanced at Karen's tense face, and added, "Not completely." I looked back at my dad. "Mostly because of *me*. Because this is my life, and I'll make the decisions. Not you. And if you can't accept that, then there's no place for you." It felt good to say the words, and even better to watch him as they sank in. More quietly I said, "I want to be a family. But not at any cost." And then I let him go and waited to see what he would do.

There was a moment when I really thought he was going to plow back into it all, and I'd have to catch him and throw him out, and I was almost wishing it would happen. It would be so much easier to just be done with all this, and if he was the one who made the decision, he'd be the one who had to take the blame. Instead, he cursed softly to himself, looking down at the blood dripping onto his shirt. And then he turned and pushed his way through the crowd, heading for the front door.

I felt softness at my shoulder and half-turned to see Karen peering up at me anxiously. "Are you okay?" she asked.

"Are you dumping me?"

"No. I'm not."

"Then I'm fine." I grinned at her, and it felt so good I smiled a little wider. "I'm better than fine."

Winslow loomed over us, then. "So, if everything's good here, maybe we should go play a little hockey? I hear that can be a fun way to spend an evening."

"Is that okay?" I asked Karen. "Whatever went wrong before, it's not going to go wrong again if I leave right now?"

She shook her head. "No. I'm good. We're good."

"Can I ask one question? Just a preview of the big important talk we'll have after the game?" She nodded, and I said, "Was this because of something my agent said? Did he do something to freak you out?"

She made a face as if trying to decide what to say, then nodded again. "Sorry, yeah. He did."

"Don't be sorry." I sure wasn't. Maybe I hadn't gotten a clean break with my dad, but this? This was much easier. I looked around until I found Brett hovering indecisively at the edge of the crowd, clearly wondering whether to do damage control with me or with my dad. "Hey, Brett," I said casually. He looked at me, a quick, oily smile on his face and it felt really good to say, "You're fired. Stay away from me, and stay the *fuck* away from my girlfriend."

And that was it. One more look at Karen, enough to earn me a wide-eyed smile, and then Winslow was clearing a path through the crowd, dragging me back to the locker room. I let it happen. In terms of people pushing me around? Winslow, okay. But anyone else? No. I was done with that.

Chapter Twenty-Eight

- *KAREN* -

"You just punched a man," Natalie said, staring at Will.

Will was looking down at his knuckles in amazement. "I guess I did, yeah." He looked back up quickly. "Sorry. I know you could have handled it yourself. You didn't need for me to do that."

She was still staring. "No, I didn't need you to," she said quietly. Then she smiled, just a little, but I could see Will notice it and I could see that it gave him hope. "But I'm not sorry you did." She looked over at me and archly raised an eyebrow. "He called me a bitch?"

I shook my head. "We don't use that word."

And that got me a smile from her, too. Then she reached over to take my hand. "You going in to watch the game? Want to sit with the family?"

"I kind of do. But Tyler might look for me, and he'd

expect me to be in the other section."

"The girlfriends' seats," she said. "No problem. But you know where we are if you need us, right?" Then she turned to look at Will. "You can sit with us, if you want."

"Yeah?"

"Yeah," she said. "We need to start talking, right? Might as well start off casual."

"Great," he said, and we all turned to walk into the seating area.

When it was time for me to branch off and go find my own seat, they both smiled and waited for me to leave, but I stopped and took a deep breath.

"Will," I said. "This might not come to anything, but if Tyler's interested… He just fired his agent, and his dad is… well, you've met his dad. But I think Tyler might need some business advice. About his parents' house, and some other stuff. He might have his own ideas, but if he doesn't? You're good at business, right? That's your thing? So, would it be okay if I suggested that he talk to you about it?"

He nodded slowly, then swallowed before saying, "Yes. Of course. I'd be honored."

Well, that was a bit more intense than I was willing to get. The whole point of asking for a favor for *Tyler* was that I wasn't quite ready to start asking for favors for myself. Not yet. But I guess Will could get worked up about weird stuff if he wanted to.

So I made my way to my seat and cheered when Tyler and the rest of the team came out on the ice, and when they got goals and whatever, and waited impatiently for the damn game to be over so Tyler and I could talk. He might have fired his agent, but that didn't automatically mean that the man hadn't had a point, after all.

Dawn and I waited for the guys in the parking lot, and when Tyler came out he hesitated just a moment before leaning in for a kiss, long enough for me to have to stretch up on my tiptoes to reach him. It felt like there was a lot riding on this kiss, somehow. When we finally pulled apart, he had his hands braced on the door of his truck on either side of my head, and he looked down at me with a strange mix of sweetness and hunger. "Do we need to talk?" he asked.

I tried to remember what words were and finally came up with, "Your agent said you need to focus on your game. He said this is a big year and you couldn't be distracted. He said... I don't know, I think he said drama could be bad for your game."

Tyler squinted at me. "So, we don't really need to talk, then."

"What? Why? I mean, I think we still do."

He shook his head. "Drama. Like today, you mean? That total rollercoaster? Drama like that?"

"Yes, exactly."

"Karen, I got two goals and three assists tonight. Did you notice that?"

"I...I guess? I mean, okay, yeah, but isn't that...is that good? I mean, I'm not stupid, I know it's *good*, but is it good enough to get you to the NHL?"

He made a frustrated sound. "It's good. I had a good game. A great game, maybe even. The drama didn't get in the way, not at all. Hockey's an emotional sport—there's nothing wrong with going into a game with a little tension built up." He kissed me gently before saying, "Was it a good enough game to get me to the NHL? I have no idea. Seriously. I can't worry about that. I just have to play my game and live my life. You know?"

"I think so." It sounded kind of like sport-speak mixed with surfer philosophy, and I wondered whether Winslow had been involved in its formulation. "Play your game, and live your life."

"And I can worry about the 'play my game' part all on my own. I'll let you know if I need help with anything, but otherwise, you don't need to worry about it. I just...I'd like it if you were involved in the 'live my life' part. I'd like you to be *heavily* involved. If that works for you."

"It does," I said. "It works for me. It really does."

And then he kissed me, and I forgot what words were for again. And I didn't care if I ever needed to use them again.

Chapter Twenty-Nine

- KAREN -

Will met with Tyler and they sorted out a plan to use Tyler's celebrity power to find a job for Tyler's dad, and it worked within, like, two days. And then Tyler and Will visited a banker friend of Will's and arranged for an extension on the MacDonald family mortgage. It was all still tight, and it depended on Tyler's dad actually showing up at work and not getting fired, but it was something, at least.

And Will started coming to the house for dinner most nights. Things could be a bit tense, but they were getting better. He and I started talking a bit more, just the two of us, and sometimes when Tyler was out of town Will would go on my morning runs with me. Not nearly as much fun as running with Tyler, and I got a bit tired of slowing myself down so Will could keep up, but he was making an effort, so I made an effort, too. Everyone was working on things, and that was okay.

One Friday night, Will and Natalie decided to go out on a date, and Miranda and Matt and Sara had their own social events, and Tyler didn't have a hockey game for a change. So he came over, and at first it was weird. We'd spent lots of time together, with and without clothes, but always either in his truck or outside. Honestly, I'd never fooled around with him in a house, and it felt weird. Like I was doing something wrong.

He called me crazy and then flopped down on the big couch in the basement. "Do you just want to watch TV, then? Or should we play backgammon or put a puzzle together, or…I'm trying to think of other things my grandparents do to pass the time."

I let myself fall, not quite on top of him but close enough to earn an "oof" before he wrapped his arm around me and pulled me in close. "We're not quite grandparently yet," I told him and kissed him in a way I hoped would prove my point.

"But clothes stay on," he said. "You're sticking with that?"

"Someone could come home any time."

"We could go out," he suggested.

"Let's stay here. I might get more comfortable soon."

"That sounds promising," he said and pulled me in for another kiss.

But I squirmed away from him instead, just far enough to pull out my phone. Tyler knew about my mom's message; we'd talked about her a bit, and I'd let him listen to it so he'd at least know what she'd sounded like.

But now I was trying something different. "I talked to Mr. Jabowski," I said slowly. He was the librarian at school and really good with technology. "He helped me download my mom's message onto my laptop, and then we backed it up in, like, fifteen different places." That had felt good, knowing that I wasn't going to have some sort of phone malfunction and lose the sound of my mother's voice forever.

"Nice," Tyler said. "You want a sixteenth place? You can store it on my computer, if you want."

"I think fifteen is probably enough. But…I think it's time to take it off my phone."

He frowned at me. "Are you sure?"

"I don't think I need it anymore. And every time I see it…" I shrugged. I'd gone to a couple sessions with a therapist, enough to know that I wanted to go to more, and most of what we'd talked about had been the process of grief. She said that for most people there came a time when they could think about a lost loved one and focus on the love and shared happiness of the past, rather than the pain. But she also said it took a long time to get to that stage. "Every time I see it I get sad," I said. "And when I listen to it, I want to go back in time." I took a deep breath. "So that's no good, because I *can't* go back in time, so I'm just wishing for something impossible and *that* makes me sad, too."

Tyler kissed my temple then pulled away just a little, keeping our heads close together. "Okay," he said. "You want help?"

It wasn't like it was all that challenging to delete a phone message, but I knew what he meant. "Can you just stay here, like this, while I do it?"

"You can always put it back on, right?"

"Yeah, as an audio file. If I need to."

So he sat there with me as I called up the message and

played it for both of us one more time. Maybe I wouldn't be seeing my mom in the morning, but I really hoped that I'd see her again sometime, somehow. I hoped I'd be able to introduce her to Tyler. I was sure she'd like him.

So I cried a little bit, and Tyler kissed my temple again and held me until I felt better. Then I squirmed around and held the phone out to him. "It's got a recorder," I said. "I want you to leave me a message. So if I think about playing hers, and it makes me sad, I can play yours, and it'll make me happy."

He looked uncertain. "I have no idea what to say."

"It doesn't matter. Just…tell me to watch out for angry squirrels, or something. It's your voice I want."

He still didn't seem completely confident, but he took the phone from my hands and looked at the screen, then punched the *record* button. He cleared his throat. "Hey, Karen. It's Tyler. You may not know it, but I'm captain of the Corrigan Falls Raiders. That's hockey. H-O-C-K-E-Y." He grinned at me, and I smiled back. This was *exactly* what I wanted to listen to before I went to sleep. "Anyway, I'm glad you asked me to record a message for you. I mean, I don't really like the recording idea, but I'm glad *I'm* the one you want a message from. Yeah." He looked at me thoughtfully, as if trying to figure out what to say next. Or maybe as if he had an idea and was trying to figure out if it was a good one. He apparently decided. "I hope this message makes you happy. I hope *I* make you happy. If I don't, please kick my ass for me, because I'm probably not screwing up on purpose and I'd really appreciate any help you could give me on being a better boyfriend. That's… It's pretty much the most important thing in the world, for me. To be the best boyfriend I can be, and to deserve to be with someone as amazing as you." Another quick look, then he gripped the phone tighter as if he'd made his final decision but was scared about it. He took a deep breath, then said, "I love you, Karen. A lot."

I stared at him. I'd been thinking about the words, but there was no way I'd been brave enough to say them. Now, he was looking at me as if waiting for something bad, which was completely ridiculous and completely Tyler. "Say it again," I whispered.

"It's recorded. You can hear it again whenever you want."

"I want you to *say* it again, right now."

He raised his eyebrows doubtfully, then nodded. "Okay. I love you."

"*With* my name," I demanded.

He finally grinned. "Seriously? You are a pain in the ass, you know that?"

"Do it!" I grabbed his wrists and even though he could have shoved me across the room without any effort, he let me guide the phone back up to his mouth. "I love you, Karen," he said as I hovered ominously over him.

"Once more," I whispered.

He nodded slowly. "Karen, I love you."

I let my arms collapse and sagged down onto him. "I love you, too," I whispered.

He caught my hair in his fist and pulled my face gently away from him. "I'm sorry," he said. "I didn't quite hear that."

I forced myself to look him in the eyes. He was just too perfect, too gorgeous, and it felt presumptuous to say the words to him. But I did it anyway. "I love you."

"And again," he said, the smirk beginning to show.

"Tyler…"

"Oh, yeah, good point," he agreed. "Use my name."

"And you say *I'm* a pain in the ass?"

"Say it," he urged quietly.

I closed my eyes, then opened them and looked down at him. "I love you, Tyler."

He let go of my hair, then, and guided my lips down to meet his.

I'd lost my mom, but I had a family of sorts, and a life, and a perfect boyfriend. Things weren't easy, but I was pretty sure they weren't supposed to be. This was the path we were running on. It wasn't a treadmill, it wasn't a carefully groomed track. We were running through the forest, and every root we jumped over, every hill we fought to climb, they all made us stronger. They made us better. Tyler and I were running a rough trail, and we liked it. And we were doing it together.

Epilogue

- *TYLER* -

Will knocked on his own front door, then pushed it open without waiting for anyone to answer. "Smells good in here," he called as I trailed inside the house behind him.

Natalie came out from the general direction of the kitchen. "How'd the meeting go?" she asked us both.

"Pretty good, I think." Will and I had debriefed in the car on the way back from meeting the latest in a string of possible agent replacements, so I knew he agreed with me. "He's got great contacts and references, and, I don't know—he seemed pretty cool." The *seemed cool* part was the only thing that was new; Will had helped me check out the references and everything before we even bothered setting up the meeting. "I think he's probably my favorite."

"Sleep on it," Will advised. "You've got lots of people who want to work with you, so don't feel like you need to make a fast decision."

I nodded. The NHL draft wasn't until the end of June, and it wasn't like I needed an agent to help me with the Raiders. And once I had someone I thought I liked, I wanted Karen to meet him before I signed anything. Will was great for the business side of things, but after the crap Brett had pulled on Karen, I wanted to be sure she was okay with anyone I was seriously considering.

And, now that I was thinking of Karen, I wanted to see her. I tried to lean around Natalie and peek into the kitchen.

"She's in the backyard," Natalie said, and her voice was softer than it had been when we were talking about agents. "I think she'll be okay, but she needed a little time alone. Holidays are hard, you know?"

I didn't know, really. I'd never lost anyone I loved. "So, if she wants to be alone, I should stay in here?" It had already felt a bit awkward having Thanksgiving dinner with Karen's family, but it was going to feel a hell of a lot weirder if she was out in the backyard the whole time.

"Oh, no, I think she'd want to see you. Go check, at least. If she still needs some space, come back in and I'll put you to work."

So I said thanks to Will one more time, then headed for the back door. Matt and Sara were in the kitchen, and Sara took a break from whatever she was doing with gourds and pine cones to give me a hug. "She's being brave," she whispered in my ear. "But she shouldn't have to be, right?"

I wasn't really sure what she meant. I mean, I understood the part about Karen being brave, and wasn't surprised to hear it. The second part, though, about how she shouldn't have to be?

Karen was my first real girlfriend, and I'll be honest—a lot of the time I didn't really know what I was doing as a boyfriend. And I don't think Karen had a much better idea of how to be a good girlfriend. I mean, we had the big picture. We knew we loved each other and we had each other's backs and we really liked spending time together. But the details? Like how to fight fair, or how to handle being jealous or whatever? We were both rookies.

And Natalie had been a really good coach for both of us. At first she'd just been talking to Karen, which made more sense, but during our first and, so far, only fight, I'd come by the house and Karen had been out for a run, and while I was waiting for her I'd helped Natalie in the garden and she and I had started talking, and everything she'd said made perfect sense. When Karen came back from running, I understood why she'd been upset—turns out girls don't really like it when their boyfriends come back from a road trip and get their truck washed instead of going straight to their girlfriends' house. And it's not because they're psycho, it's because they want to feel like a priority. It made sense, once Natalie pointed it out to me.

So I'd started talking to Natalie more. About my family, and hockey and stuff, not just Karen. Most of the time Karen was there, and sometimes Sara was, too. And Sara was kind of a junior Natalie, with lots of wisdom and good advice, but at the same time, she was a fourteen-year-old kid, and sometimes she didn't really know what she was talking about. My problem came from telling which was which.

So that last little bit about how Karen shouldn't have to be brave? I wasn't sure if it was wisdom or random. But there was really only one good way to find out, so I kept going, out the back door into the cool fall air.

Karen was sitting on a wooden bench at the far end of the garden, her back toward the house. At least she was still in the yard, not down at the park or something. That was probably a good sign.

I shuffled my feet through the dry leaves on the ground when I got close to her, giving her a little warning. "You okay?" I asked.

She spun around a little too fast. "I'm fine." For a second, I thought that's all I was going to get, but then she frowned. Not like she was mad, but like she was trying to order herself to not cry. "It's stupid."

"Probably not," I said cautiously and took a few more steps forward. "You want to tell me about it?"

"No, because then you'll think I'm stupid." She grinned a little, but it was pretty weak around the edges and didn't last as long as it should have.

"I bet I don't."

She gave me a long look. "I got sad because they put beets in their roasted root vegetable medley."

Possibly I was going to have a bit of backtracking to do on the *not stupid* front. "That made you sad?"

She nodded. "Because my mom and I hate beets. Stupid, right? I mean, they asked if I had any favorite Thanksgiving foods, and I said I loved roasted root vegetables. You know, potatoes and turnips and carrots and parsnips…"

"But not beets."

"And they were so nice!" She was crying a little, now. "They said they'd add the root vegetables to their menu, and then when I came upstairs to help they'd already started, and there were beets in with all the *good* root vegetables.

And it just—" She stopped then brushed her tears away impatiently. "Stupid, right?"

"No," I said. It only took me one step to make it the rest of the way to the bench, and I sank down beside her and twined my fingers through hers. "It's not stupid. Beets are gross."

She snorted a little, then tightened her fingers around mine. "It's not really about the beets."

"I know. You miss your mom. I get it."

"And I don't want to—I mean, things are a bit weird already, with Will and Natalie, and Miranda still isn't crazy about you being around, and they're all trying so hard to be happy, and I don't want to wreck it with stupid blubbering about something nobody can do anything to fix."

"You can pick them out," I told her. "That's the best thing about beets—they're easy to spot."

The snort was closer to a laugh this time. "Oh, okay then. Problem solved."

I wrapped my arm around her shoulder and squeezed, and she relaxed against me, snaking her arm around my waist, under my jacket. "You're right. Nobody can do anything to fix the big problem. There's nothing we can do about your mom being gone." And then I understood what Sara had meant in the kitchen. "But I don't think you have to hide from them. I think it's okay if they know you're a bit sad. You don't have to be brave with them, maybe? Because they're your family now, and family is who you can be a little weak around, if you have to be."

Her cheek was wet but warm as she burrowed it in against my neck. "That's what I have you for." She pulled away a little and turned her head so she could see me.

"Unless you're getting tired of it?"

My turn to twist around so I could kiss her forehead. "I'm not tired of it. And if I'm around, I'm happy to be sad with you for a while. No problem. But if I'm not around? I think they'd be okay with it. Really."

We sat there quietly for a while. Then she said, "You want me to tell them they're stupid for putting beets in the root vegetable medley?"

"I think you could probably leave the beets out of the conversation."

"I wish they'd left the beets out of the medley."

I kissed her again, this time on the top of her head. "It's not about the beets, babe."

We sat there quietly for a while longer, then Karen groaned and pushed herself away from me. "We should go in." She brushed at her cheeks with her hands. "Do I look okay?"

"You look good. But even if you didn't?"

She nodded slowly. "Yeah, okay. Even if I didn't, I could go in. They're family. I don't have to be brave." She frowned at me. "Wait. Who do *you* not have to be brave around? Besides me?"

"The team, mostly." I looked toward the house and shrugged. "But in terms of family? I think I'm kind of stealing yours a bit. That okay?"

"We can share." She stood up and held out her hand, and when I took it she tugged me to my feet. "Come on. The beets are going to get cold."

So we headed for the house, our hands locked tight together. It was Karen's first Thanksgiving without her mom, and I didn't think any of us would expect her to forget that.

But I was pretty sure we could remind her that there were some good firsts, too. Her first holiday with her new family, and with me. The first of many.

"You're okay?" I asked her as her hand reached for the door handle.

She paused, turned to me, and gave me a kiss that promised more later. "I'm good," she said. "You?"

"I'm good, too."

"Okay. Let's go be good together."

And that's what we did. But neither one of us ate the beets.

About the Author

Cate Cameron grew up in the city but moved to the country in her mid-twenties and isn't looking back. Most of her writing deals with people living and loving in small towns or right out in the sticks—when there aren't entertainment options on every corner, other people get a lot more interesting!

She likes to write stories about real people struggling with real issues. YA, NA, or contemporary romance, her books are connected by their emphasis on subtle humor and characters who are trying to do the right thing, even when it would be a lot easier to do something wrong.

Sneak peek of book two, *Playing Defense*

CHAPTER ONE

"Claudia, you should have more extracurriculars," Mrs. Davidson said firmly. She was the school's guidance counselor and said almost *everything* firmly. "Your marks are excellent, and they'll *probably* be enough to get you in to most schools. But you want more than 'probably', don't you?"

I absolutely wanted more than *probably*, and I wanted more than *most schools*, too. I was looking for guaranteed acceptance to the engineering program at the University of Waterloo, the best engineering school in the country. That was my goal, and I was *very* goal oriented. But there had to be some other way to reach it. "Maybe I should look at the list again," I suggested. I wasn't athletic, and the school didn't offer much besides sports, but there had to be something.

Something that *wasn't* what she was suggesting.

Mrs. Davidson handed the sheet of paper across her desk again. "We're a small school," she said. I wasn't sure if she was trying to be soothing, apologetic, or just realistic. "There are limited options. Student government is already filled up, and you said you weren't interested in the environment. So tutoring is a good option for you."

Okay, for the record, it's not like I hate the environment. I'm interested in it. I'm an environmentalist, even. But the club at our school was fairly radical; they were always talking about making a stand and getting arrested in the name of progress and a lot of other things that would *not* appeal to my dream school. So the Young Environmentalists club was out. "I just don't think I'd be all that good at tutoring," I tried.

"That's unfortunate. A lot of schools—Waterloo included—are looking for students who are strong communicators as well as strong calculators. Taking part in tutoring would show that you can share your knowledge, not just accumulate it."

Maybe it's because I'm an only child, but I'm really not that big on sharing. Unfortunately, it wasn't looking like I had much choice. "Okay," I sighed. "Tutoring. Alicia's doing that thing with the elementary students—is that where you'd put me?"

"Well, no," Mrs. Davidson said. "That program is full, and we actually have a need a little closer to home. A senior student is having some trouble with advanced functions *and* chemistry. With your excellence in both subjects, I think you'd really be able to help him out."

I squinted at her suspiciously. "*Which* senior student?"

Her smile was too bland to be trusted. "Chris Winslow. Do you know him?"

Like she'd said, it was a small school. But even if it had been bigger, I still would have known Chris Winslow. He was pretty impossible to overlook. "The hockey player?" I squeaked.

She looked down at her papers really quickly, but not fast enough to keep me from seeing her smirk. She was enjoying this.

I wasn't. "I really don't think I'd do well with Chris Winslow. I mean, he's—he needs— I don't think—"

"You'll do very well," Mrs. Davidson said firmly. "The world is made of all kinds of people, and to be successful in it you'll need to learn how to get along with everyone, not just with others who are serious and academically inclined."

"Okay, so that's something I should work toward. Fine. But baby steps, right? I mean, going from 'serious and academically inclined' to *Chris Winslow*? That's a pretty extreme transition!"

"You've been resisting all my efforts at 'baby steps' for over three years. You only have eight months left in your high school career. Eight more months to try things out while you still have a safety net. Once you leave this school, and this town, you'll find that people are much less forgiving. This is your chance, Claudia. I suggest you take it."

"Chris Winslow," I said dully. "Functions and chemistry." Then I saw my way out. "He'll never agree to it. All he cares about is hockey, and girls, and beer, and goofing around with his friends. He's not going to want a tutor."

"He's the one who asked me for help," Mrs. Robinson said gently. She glanced out her window as if something had caught her eye, then stood up from behind her desk and eased past the filing cabinet to get a better look at whatever it was. "Oh," she said.

I stood up, too, and looked over her shoulder. "Holy... well. Holy cow," I said.

She turned to look at me. "Indeed." She took a deep breath and gusted it out like she was doing a breathing exercise. "Could you please go find the principal and let her know about this? I'll go down and try to... I'm not quite sure. Try to control the situation."

"Yeah, okay," I said, and started for the door. It had been strange to see a small herd of cattle on the school's front lawn. Stranger still to realize that they weren't the usual black and white kind. Instead, these cattle were black and yellow. Brilliant, almost neon yellow.

Someone had dyed them. And it probably wasn't just a coincidence that the local hockey team's colors were black and yellow. Probably not a coincidence at all.

· · ·

It was really hard to pay attention to whatever Dr. Stanis was talking about. I mean, it was *always* hard to pay attention to her—she was nice and everything, and clearly really into her subject, but math just wasn't my thing. It didn't matter how excited she got about it—it was still all just random numbers and symbols to me. So even on a good day, it was hard to keep my mind on her lessons. But on *this* day? Pretty much impossible.

We'd rigged up cameras, of course. Two phones propped up on the dashboards of cars parked by the front lawn, and a video camera taped outside the window of the second floor history classroom. I was stuck on the opposite side of the building, so I couldn't actually see any of it live, but the guys with classes facing the front had promised to record as much of it as they could, once they were done playing innocent and were able to join the crowd of onlookers. So I'd be able to watch it all, eventually. But I wanted to know what was going on *right then*.

"Chris?" Dr. Stanis said gently. I hadn't even realized she'd been standing next to me. Hadn't realized she'd left the front of the classroom and was circulating around, offering help. "What's the first step going to be?"

I looked down at the numbers I'd copied off the board, then up at her. "Maybe I should make another guidance appointment? Maybe I could take a tech instead."

She shook her head. "You can do this, Chris. And if you want to go to university instead of community college, you *will* do this. You'll at least pass this course. But you need to try."

I nodded. We'd had this conversation before. This was actually her second year as my math teacher, so you'd think she'd have a pretty good understanding of my ability. Or my *lack* of ability, more like it. But she was an optimist. I guess for someone as smart as her, it would be pretty hard to understand how someone else could be so stupid. "Yeah," I said, because there wasn't much else *to* say.

But I wasn't getting rid of her that easily. She pointed at the page again. "So. What's the first step going to be?"

I stared at the page. Integration by substitution. That was what we were doing. Integration by substitution. I figured I had a fifty-fifty chance of being right. "We substitute?"

She didn't answer right away, so I quickly said, "No, we integrate?"

"How do we know if we even *need* to substitute?" she asked patiently.

"Oh, the list!"

"Good, yes. Is this function on the list?"

"Give me a minute," I said, and started sorting through my notes. There was a list of functions, somewhere, somewhere…

"Find the list, see if this function fits, and I'll be back after I help Amanda," she said and left my desk to go harass the girl a couple rows over. Not that she was harassing. She was helping, or trying to. But she didn't seem to realize just how hopeless I was.

My phone vibrated then. We weren't supposed to have them in class, but short of a full-body search, there was no way to keep students from carrying them in. But if I got caught looking at it, Dr. Stanis would take it away, and it'd be a pain to get it back. So I eased it out of my back pocket and glanced at it in my lap.

The text was from Tyler MacDonald, who'd been my best friend ever since we both came to Corrigan Falls to play hockey. *There are yellow and black cows at school*, it read.

A second later, the phone vibrated again. *Tell me u didn't have anything to do with this.*

Yeah, Tyler was my best friend, but he was pretty serious. When I pulled pranks, I left him out of it.

I glanced at the teacher to be sure she was still busy and quickly texted, *Stop distracting me. I'm trying to learn.*

There was no response, but I could picture Tyler's frustration all the same. Too mad to type, probably.

I grinned, and the bell finally rang, and clearly I wasn't

the only one who'd been doing a little undercover texting because the whole class surged for the door and headed toward the front of the school.

I know, they're just cows. Really not that exciting. But Corrigan Falls is a pretty quiet place, except on game nights. So livestock at school, especially when the livestock was wearing Raiders colors, was worth seeing.

I worked my way out of the school and toward the front of the crowd, even though I was tall enough to have a pretty good view from the back, and found Tyler wrapped around Karen, his girlfriend, both of them watching the cows like they thought the animals might start doing tricks. When Tyler saw me coming, he shook his head. "If you get caught for this, Coach will bench you. Guaranteed."

"Of course I don't know what you're talking about," I said.

"Of course," Karen agreed. She was smirking a little, so I figured Tyler couldn't be all that mad. The two of them are usually on the same wavelength about things.

Then Karen's eyes widened a little, and she turned back to the cows really quickly. I wasn't too surprised when I heard a familiar voice from beside me.

"Chris," Mrs. Davidson said. She was pretty cool, as guidance counselors go, but probably not cool enough to really appreciate my genius on this one.

So I gave her my best innocent look. "Hey, Mrs. Davidson! Cows!"

"Yes. Cows."

Damn. She had a pretty good stare, like she could see right through me, right into my nasty little prank-pulling soul. But she couldn't get me in trouble if her only evidence was soul-vision. "Where'd they come from?" I asked, still innocent.

She sighed. "That's an excellent question, Chris. Where *did* they come from?"

She asked like she really wanted to know, but I wasn't going to get sucked in that easily. Still, it wouldn't hurt to help her out a little. "There's a dairy farm just past the trees, isn't there? I wonder if they came from over there. Maybe they broke through the fence."

"Broke through the fence and dyed themselves yellow?"

"Well, I guess probably they didn't dye themselves, no."

"So maybe somebody *helped them* through the fence."

"Huh. Well, yeah, I guess. You're probably right." Some people like being told that they're right, but apparently Mrs. Davidson wasn't one of them, because her expression was still stony.

"I wonder what they were dyed *with*," she said.

I frowned. "I bet it's something safe. Like, something that wouldn't hurt them. Probably food coloring." I turned to Tyler. He'd be pissed off, but he'd back me up. We were teammates. "Does that look like food coloring to you, Mac?"

He gave me a dirty look but then nodded grumpily. "Probably just food coloring, yeah."

"And I wonder why they're all collected on the lawn like they are," Mrs. Davidson said. "Seems like cattle would usually roam around a little, doesn't it?"

"Maybe there's some sort of mystical force at work," I suggested, but she didn't seem impressed. "Or maybe somebody poured something on the grass to make it taste better. Sugar, or salt, or… I don't know, Ms. Walker, I really couldn't tell you much about what cows like to eat. But maybe there's some of whatever it is on the grass right there."

"Maybe there was a path of it leading in from the forest," Karen said. She hadn't been part of the prank, but she was clearly having fun with the cover up. "Somebody could have come last night and laid a path, and probably nobody would have noticed it this morning." She looked from Mrs. Davidson to me. "Right?"

"I don't know," I said firmly. We all needed to remember that I didn't know. "But I guess that would make sense, yeah."

"Can I see your hands, Chris?" Mrs. Davidson said. Not aggressive or anything, just like she was a little curious.

So I lifted my hands. Clean and pink, no trace of artificial yellow. "I don't know if you'll be able to catch people that way," I said. "Probably whoever did it would have worn gloves, right?"

"Right," she said. Then she smiled. "Chris, you're a leader at this school, aren't you?"

"A leader? Uh—"

"Yes, you are. Don't be modest. And I think as a leader, you need to take some responsibility for things that happen here, don't you?"

"Take responsibility? Like how?"

"Like getting these cows back where they belong. Making sure the fence is in good repair. I'll drive over and let the farmer know what's going on, and I'll ask him to put out buckets and a hose and some rags so you can wash these cows and get them back to their natural color. You can take the cattle back now, on your lunch hour, and wash them after school today."

"Oh, no, I can't. I mean, the lunchtime thing, sure, I can do that. But after school today I have practice. Maybe we could just wait until it rains on them?"

"I don't think the farmer should be asked to milk black and yellow cows until the next time it rains. I'll call your coach and let him know why you can't make practice."

That didn't sound like a good idea at all. "Uh…well, Tyler can probably tell him. I know how busy you are, and Coach can be really hard to get hold of. You don't need to worry about it."

She raised an eyebrow. "I have his cell number, Chris. I speak to him fairly regularly. I've never found him hard to get hold of."

"Huh. Well…he must really like you. That's nice, isn't it? He answers your calls when he won't pick up for his own players."

"So he'll be happy to hear from me, even if I'm giving him some bad news."

This wasn't going well at all. "Wait. Bad news? Just that I'm late for practice today. That's all. You're not going to tell him something *else*, are you?"

"Well, I should possibly talk to him about your marks, too."

This conversation was going in a lot of different directions, none of which seemed good. "Uh, wait. You said you'd set up a tutor." I'd asked her if I could just drop functions and chemistry, but the school's so small there isn't a lot of choice in any given period. She couldn't find a way to make my schedule work without those courses, not if I still wanted to get the credits I needed to go to university. Which I still kind of did, even if I *was* pretty sure I'd end up flunking out in my first year.

"That's right, you *did* ask for a tutor—that was very

responsible of you. And I think I have someone in mind. But I don't want to waste her time if you aren't committed. So, Chris, I need to know you're going to follow through with it."

Well, she knew me pretty well. "I plan to," I told her honestly.

She smiled, but her eyes were sharp. "I think I'd like a little more than that, Chris. Tell you what. These cows get home safely and get washed, *and* I get good reports from your tutor that you're making a genuine effort? And I'll hold off on calling the coach. But any problems with the cows, *or* with the tutoring? I'll not only call him, I'll ask him to bench you until your attitude improves. Clear?"

"But—the cows—you don't—that could have been anybody!"

"I am cruel and unfair. If you want to complain about it, give your parents a call; I'd be pleased to discuss the situation with them. Or with the coach." She waited just long enough to make it clear that she'd called my bluff and I had no more arguments to make. Then she smiled. "Okay. So I'll hear good things about clean cows and tutoring. And if I don't…."

She didn't really need to finish the threat, and we both knew it. So she turned and walked away, and I stared glumly at the cows.

"Git along, lil' doggie," Tyler told me.

"Doggies are cows, not cowboys."

"Okay, then, giddyup. Whatever. Get the cows home and start washing them. I'll round up the guys and we'll come help. Maybe we can get it done fast and you won't miss practice."

"Yeah?"

Tyler shrugged. "You're an idiot, but you're *our* idiot. We'll help."

So I started rounding up the cattle; they'd finished licking up the sugar-water we'd sprayed all over the grass so they weren't as hard to move as they might have been a bit earlier. And there were quite a few farm kids in the crowd who were happy to show off skills that usually didn't get a whole lot of attention at school. So we had a nice little parade heading across the lawn, over the driveway, and into the forest on the far side. The cattle didn't seem to care too much about staying on the path, so it got a bit hard to keep track of them, but we finally made it back to the fence we'd cut and carefully re-wired to make sure no extra cows escaped while these ones were on vacation. I noticed that the other guys who had helped me with the prank weren't helping with the clean-up; maybe they were collecting the video evidence, or maybe they were just goofing off. I was the only one of us who had hockey to be taken away, so I was the only one who really cared about staying out of trouble.

Besides, I didn't want the cows to get hurt, *or* the farmer to get pissed off. It had always been the plan to return them.

It was the washing that I hadn't really counted on.

But as I looked toward the barn, I saw a group of kids waiting for us. There must have been fifty people, way more than were on the hockey team. That was the thing about Tyler: people just wanted to follow him, even if he was doing something as stupid as washing food coloring off cows.

I wasn't going to complain about the help, that was for sure. We divided up the rags and the buckets and set up a sort of conveyer-belt of cows, each animal being led along past a gang of kids scrubbing different parts, then rinsed off by the guys with the hoses at the end.

It was October, but a pretty warm day, so it really wasn't that bad to be out there in the sun with my friends. And the farmer was a Raiders fan, just like practically everyone else in town, so he thought the whole thing was hilarious.

Overall, I was in a pretty good mood as we finished off with the cows and trooped back through the woods toward the school, only a few minutes late for our after-lunch classes. A bit stinky, because wet cows smell about as good as wet dogs, but that was kind of a badge of honor.

Of course, Tyler couldn't just let me enjoy the moment. "You need to do the tutoring," he said as he walked along beside me. "The cows were easy, but Mrs. Davidson isn't going to forget about the rest of it. And you know how Coach will react if she calls him."

Yeah, I knew. Coach cared about hockey, sure, but it wasn't *all* he cared about. Unfortunately. I'd seen him bench guys before, not letting them play until they got their marks up, and I was hoping that this would be my final season in the league. I needed to be on the ice if I was going to get the scouts to notice me. "I'll do it," I grumbled.

"Yeah, you will," Tyler said. He sounded almost threatening. "I'll make sure of it."

Sometimes he took the team captain job a bit too seriously. But, still, I guess it was nice to have him on my side. Nice that he cared enough to nag. I guess.

CPSIA information can be obtained
at www.ICGtesting.com
Printed in the USA
LVOW04s0531191216
517897LV00008B/750/P